Leila stood and exhaled sh̶̶ ̶ ̶ ̶ ̶ ̶ ̶ ̶ ̶ ̶ ̶ ̶ *e*
her by the hand to ̶ ̶ ̶ ̶ ̶ ̶ ̶ ̶ ̶ ̶ ̶ ̶ ̶ ̶ ̶ ̶ ̶
gave another shak̶ ̶ ̶ ̶ ̶ ̶ ̶ ̶ ̶ ̶ ̶ ̶ ̶ ̶ ̶ ̶ ̶ ̶ ̶
pressed her close. ̶ ̶ ̶ ̶ ̶ ̶ ̶ ̶ ̶ ̶ ̶ ̶ ̶ ̶ ̶ *t*
dirty dancing. She ̶ ̶ ̶ ̶ ̶ ̶ ̶ ̶ ̶ ̶ ̶ ̶ ̶ ̶ ̶ ̶
maybe that was too̶ ̶ ̶ ̶ ̶ *ent. Heat was*
rampaging through her as she came into contact
with every alarming contour of his body.

"I thought you wanted to dance," Raffa prompted when she remained quite still.

"*You* wanted to dance," she reminded him, reluctant to end her sensory exploration of a man who was every bit as hard as he looked.

"Yes. With you," he confirmed, tightening his grip.

Raffa didn't take no for an answer, Leila discovered as he swept her round the floor.

"I like your style, Leila Skavanga," he murmured, his voice all husky and rough.

"Really?" She prepared herself for some glowing compliment from the master of charm. "Why?"

"Stubborn. Tricky. Unpredictable." Raffa shrugged. "I never know what to expect from you."

Then he wouldn't be surprised when her stiletto hit his foot.

"What's wrong now, Leila?"

She sniffed. "I'm waiting for the right beat of the music."

"Ah, a perfectionist."

"No. A novice."

"A novice?" Raffa's warm breath brushed her ear. "I could soon change that."

All about the author...
Susan Stephens

SUSAN STEPHENS was a professional singer before meeting her husband on the tiny Mediterranean island of Malta. In true Harlequin Presents® style, they met on Monday, became engaged on Friday and were married three months later. Almost thirty years and three children later, they are still in love. (Susan does not advise her children to return home one day with a similar story, as she may not take the news with the same fortitude as her own mother!)

Susan had written several nonfiction books when fate took a hand. At a charity costume ball there was an after-dinner auction. One of the lots, "Spend a Day with an Author," had been donated by Harlequin Presents author Penny Jordan. Susan's husband bought this lot, and Penny was to become not just a great friend, but a wonderful mentor who encouraged Susan to write romance.

Susan loves her family, her pets, her friends and her writing. She enjoys entertaining, travel and going to the theater. She reads, cooks and plays the piano to relax, and can occasionally be found throwing herself off mountains on a pair of skis or galloping through the countryside.

Visit Susan's website, www.susanstephens.net. She loves to hear from her readers all around the world!

Other titles by Susan Stephens available in ebook:

THE FLAW IN HIS DIAMOND (Skavanga Diamonds)
DIAMOND IN THE DESERT
TAMING THE LAST ACOSTA
THE ARGENTINIAN'S SOLACE

Susan Stephens

The Purest of Diamonds?

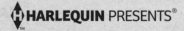

Recycling programs
for this product may
not exist in your area.

ISBN-13: 978-0-373-13235-5

THE PUREST OF DIAMONDS?

First North American Publication 2014

Copyright © 2014 by Susan Stephens

Printed in U.S.A.   www.Harlequin.com

The Purest of Diamonds?

For Fiona, Blogger and Tweeter extraordinaire. Your enthusiasm for romance makes writing sheer pleasure.

CHAPTER ONE

TENSION COILED IN Leila's stomach as she peered out of the cab window to weigh up the party guests pouring into the hotel. This time of year wasn't great for holding an event in the frozen north. Leila's home town of Skavanga was beyond the Arctic Circle in the land of the midnight sun, but when her sister Britt threw a party no one cared about the weather. Sky-high heels and bodycon was the order of the day for the women, while the men rocked formal suits beneath their silk scarves and alpaca overcoats. The mantra for the packs of girls heading up the steps to the hotel appeared to be: if you're going to freeze, do it on the way to Britt's party.

Leila was the only one of three Skavanga sisters who didn't shine at parties. Small talk wasn't her strength. She was happiest in her office in the basement of the mining museum, gathering and recording fascinating information—

Relax, Leila instructed herself firmly. Britt had lent her a gorgeous dress with a pair of spindle-heeled sandals to match, and she had a fleece-lined jacket sitting next to her in the cab. All she had to do was run up the steps of the hotel, breeze into the lobby and get lost in the crush.

'You have a good time now!' the cabbie insisted as she

paid the fare, adding a hefty tip because she felt sorry for him having to work such a filthy night.

'Sorry I couldn't get you any closer to the hotel,' he added, pulling a long face. 'I've never seen so many cabs here before—'

The Britt effect, Leila thought as she smiled. 'Don't worry. This is fine for me—'

'Careful you don't slip, love—'

Too late!

'You all right?' The cab driver leaned out of his open window to take a look at her.

'Fine, thank you.'

Liar. She had just performed a series of skating moves that would have done any ice star proud—if that ice star were a clown, that was.

The cabbie shook his head with concern. 'The roads are really icy tonight.'

She'd noticed. She was currently lodged in an inelegant squatting position at the side of his cab, her tights were ripped, and her dress was…thankfully not completely ruined after a close encounter with the side of a mud-streaked cab. Thank goodness her dress was blue-black. Navy was a great colour. It could be sponged.

Picking herself up, she stood waiting for a gap in the traffic. The cabbie was also waiting for the cars to clear. 'Aren't those the three men in the consortium that saved the town?' he said, pointing.

Leila's heart lurched. Sure enough, heading in arrow formation up the steps of the hotel were her elder sister Britt's husband, the Sheikh of Kareshi; her middle sister Eva's fiancé, the impossibly handsome Italian Count Roman Quisvada; and the third man in the consortium, who drew her gaze like a heat-seeking missile to its target. Powering up the steps ahead of the other men, Raffa Leon. Dangerously attractive. Currently single.

Turning away from more trouble than most women could handle, Leila shook her head with impatience for allowing herself to indulge in a moment of sheer fantasy. She was the shy, virginal sister in a family of out-there go-getters, and Raffa spelled danger in any language. Even the most experienced woman would think twice before falling into his lap, and she was more of a small-town mouse.

But the cabbie was right in saying the three men had saved the town. Leila and her two sisters, Britt and Eva, along with their long-lost brother, Tyr, had used to own the Skavanga mine outright, but when the minerals ran out and diamonds were discovered, they couldn't afford the specialized equipment required to mine the precious stones. The town of Skavanga had always depended on the mine for its existence, so the future of everyone who lived there had been at stake too. It had been such a relief when the powerful consortium had moved in, saving both the business and the town.

'There's one billionaire left, if you hurry,' the cabbie commented with a wink. 'The other two are married—or about to be, I heard.'

'Yes.' Leila smiled. 'To my sisters—'

'So you're one of the famous Skavanga Diamonds,' the cabbie exclaimed, clearly impressed.

'That's what they call us,' Leila admitted. She laughed. 'I'm the smallest stone with the most flaws—'

'Which makes you the most interesting in my book,' the cabbie cut in. 'And you're still in with a chance, seeing as there's one billionaire left for you.'

She loved his sense of humour and couldn't stop herself laughing. 'I've got more sense than that,' she as-

sured him. 'And I'm definitely not Raffa Leon's type.'
She gave a theatrical sigh. 'Thank goodness.'

'He has got a bit of a reputation,' the cabbie agreed.
'But you don't want to believe everything you read about
people in the press.'

Remembering how the glossies made out that all three
Skavanga sisters were currently monopolising the world
stage, at least as far as celebrity went, Leila was inclined
to believe him. The only stage she stood a chance of
monopolising was the bus shelter on her way to work.

'And remember this,' the cabbie added, giving Leila
an appraising look. 'Billionaires like to marry down.
They want a quiet life at home. They have enough excitement in the office. Don't take offence,' he said quickly.
'I mean that as a compliment. You look like a nice, quiet
girl, is all.'

By this point Leila was convulsed with laughter. 'And
no offence taken. Now *you* be careful of the icy roads.
I'm guessing you've got a long, cold night ahead of you.'

'Too right, I have. Goodnight, love. You have fun at
that party.'

'I will,' she promised. Just as soon as she had visited
the restroom to sort out her dress. Parties might not be
her thing, but she had no intention of letting down her
glamorous sisters by arriving at their celebration looking as if she'd been mud wrestling before she arrived.

Picking her way carefully across the icy road as soon
as there was a gap in the traffic, she launched herself
into the shadows. Raffa Leon was standing at the top of
the steps scanning the street, probably waiting for some
glamorous socialite to decant from a limo.

God, he was gorgeous!

But bang went her plan for an anonymous entrance—
Not necessarily... All she had to do was choose

her moment and scoot past him. He wouldn't even notice her—

Wrong.

Everything was going so well. Raffa was looking one
way while she was running up the steps on his blind side.
But then she hit a patch of ice, and while her heels went
one way she went the other. With a shriek, she prepared
to hit the stone hard.

Wrong again.

'Leila Skavanga!'

She was shocked into silence for a moment as the
most impossibly handsome face in the world hovered
inches from her own.

'Raffa Leon!' She faked surprise. 'Goodness! Please
forgive me. I didn't see you standing there—'

Much.

Surprise? Make that *deeply* embarrassing. If there
was one lap she didn't want to land in tonight, it was
this lap. And Raffa was holding her so firmly she had
no option but to remain exactly where she was, with him
shooting heat through her veins, and quite a lot of other
places too. Trying not to breathe in case the cheese sandwich she'd chomped down earlier overrode the smell of
toothpaste, she remained immobile, while he...while he
just smelled amazing. *And those eyes...*

'Thank you,' she said, recovering her senses as he
lifted her and steadied her on her feet.

'I'm glad I caught you.'

His voice was deep and sexy, and faintly accented
in a way that would have made the call of a corncrake
sound melodious. 'I'm glad you did too.' He had just
performed a save that would have earned him a standing ovation if she'd been a rugby ball.

'You didn't twist your ankle, did you?'

The man for whom the phrase tall, dark and hand-some had been invented was looking at her legs. Deeply conscious of her ruined tights, she made a big play of brushing herself down. 'No. I'm fine.' She shook both feet in turn as if to prove the point and then felt stupid. He made her feel so gauche.

'We have met before,' he said, easing his big, sexy shoulders in a shrug.

'In the reception line at Britt's wedding,' she con-firmed. 'It's good to see you again.'

Not only did he smell divine, and he was unreason-ably compelling in a swarthy, piratical way, but those wicked eyes and that energy flying off him, both were off the scale. This encounter was so far out of her com-fort zone, it was embarrassing, and she was longing to escape, but Raffa seemed in no hurry to get away. In fact he was studying her face as if she were one of the exhibits in the museum. Was her mascara smudged? She wasn't very good at applying make-up. Worse! Did she have sandwich stuck in her teeth?

Closing her mouth, she checked discreetly with her tongue.

'Not only did we meet before, we're almost family, Leila.'

'Sorry…' When Raffa's eyes smiled into hers, she couldn't think straight. 'Family?'

'*Sí,*' Raffa insisted in his addictive Spanish drawl. 'Now the second member of the consortium is marry-ing a Skavanga sister, there's only us two left. There's no need to look so shocked, Señorita Skavanga. I only meant that perhaps we can get to know each other a lit-tle better now.'

Did he really want to?

Why did he want to?

Instantly suspicious of why such a devastatingly successful, good-looking man would want to get to know her better, she blurted, 'I don't have many shares in the company.'

Raffa laughed then forced a gasp out of her as he bowed over her hand. 'I don't have any intention of stealing your shares, Leila.'

How could someone brushing his lips over the back of her hand cause so much sensation? She'd read about things like this. Before they were married or engaged her sisters had talked incessantly about romantic encounters, but this was a whole new world for Leila. Not that Raffa meant to be romantic. It was just his way of putting her at ease.

So why was it having the opposite effect?

People were still pouring up the steps to the party, pressing in on them from every side, making conversation impossible, let alone making it easy to move away from each other. And she was hopeless at small talk. The weather? It was always cold in Skavanga. That would keep them talking for all of ten seconds. But this was a Skavanga sisters' party, and Raffa was their guest, so it was up to her to make him feel welcome.

Bracing herself, she launched in. 'I hope you're enjoying your trip to Skavanga.'

He seemed amused by her opening sally. 'I am now.'

This was accompanied by a slanting smile that would bring Hollywood to its knees.

'It's been back-to-back business meetings for me before tonight,' he explained, his face turning serious, which was another great look for him. 'I just finished another meeting.'

'So you're staying here at the hotel?'

She blushed as Raffa held her gaze and frowned

slightly. He probably thought she was coming on to him, when that was a typical example of Leila Skavanga out of her depth and swimming frantically to reach the shore. Or, to put it another way: she had zero small talk.

Fortunately, Raffa had turned to assess the logistics of making it through the door without being trampled on. 'It seems to have quietened down a bit. Shall we go in?'

'Oh, I can make it from here,' she insisted, guessing he was longing to get away.

'Don't look so worried, Leila,' he said, smiling. 'You're going to love the party. Trust me...'

Trust Raffa Leon? When everyone knew his reputation? 'I'd better find my sisters, but thank you for your assurance—and for your great save,' she added as an afterthought, smiling.

'Don't mention it.'

His eyes were warm and luminous, and they plumbed deep, considering Raffa Leon was practically a stranger. This only made her more determined to stick to her original plan, which was to share a quick drink with her sisters, eat dinner—without spilling food down her, if possible—and then indulge in a little non-controversial chit-chat before shooting off as soon as she politely could.

'You're shivering, Leila—'

Oh... She was, she realised now.

'And you're laughing?'

She bit her lip, to stop thinking about the Raffa effect, and how her shivering had nothing to do with the freezing cold.

'Here—put my overcoat on...'

'Oh, no, I—'

Too late! She might have a perfectly good jacket, but Raffa's reflexes were too fast for her and now she had his coat draped round her shoulders. It was hard to pretend she wasn't distracted by his residual heat in the coat, or by the fact that it still carried the faint imprint of his cologne.

'How did you get all this mud on your dress, Leila?'

As he noticed everything she decided to make a joke of it. 'I…um…slipped away for a minute?'

He laughed. 'And I thought I saved you.'

'Almost.'

'Next time I'll have to do better.'

'Hopefully, there won't be a next time. It was my fault for chatting to the cabbie instead of looking where I was going.'

Raffa's mouth kicked up at one corner as his eyes lit in a conspiratorial smile. 'The landing wasn't too hard, I hope?'

It was hard not to laugh. 'Only my pride got bruised.'

'I think we'd better go inside before you have another accident, don't you, Leila?'

His smile was indefensibly sexy, she concluded, dragging her gaze away, but it was nice to have a man take care of her for once, especially when she was Ms Independence—not that she was going to make a habit of it, but for a few short minutes on this one special night, it couldn't hurt to lap up his aura, and she was quite sure Don Leon would find some excuse or other to part company as soon as they were inside the hotel.

So, he'd finally met the third Skavanga sister. And for longer than a ten-second handshake in a receiving line. She had turned out to be quite a surprise. Tense, but funny, Leila Skavanga was hugely lacking in self-confidence for some reason. He didn't blame her for not relishing the prospect of a party—false smiles and meaningless chit-chat weren't his favourite form of recreation either.

It was hard being the youngest in a family, as he knew only too well, though he'd broken free of the constraints imposed on him at a young age. When he'd been young, with absentee parents, and three older brothers to kick him around, not to mention two older sisters, who took great pleasure finishing the job, it was no surprise he'd turned out to be a handful. In his experience you went one of two ways as the youngest child: determined and driven, as he was, or retiring and apologetic, like Leila Skavanga.

'Let's find the restroom first, to sort out your clothes,' he suggested as soon as they were inside the hotel. He was feeling unusually protective towards this woman, he realised as Leila glanced at him.

'That was my plan,' she confirmed as if to let him know that she was setting the ground rules—and she could look after herself, thank you very much.

'Before I intercepted you?'

'Before I landed in your lap,' she corrected him.

He laughed into her eyes. He liked the defiance he saw there. There was more to Leila Skavanga than met the eye. But then her cheeks flushed red and she looked away.

Why was she embarrassed? Too much physical contact? Too much physical contact with him?

Could Leila really be that innocent? His ingénue radar—rusty from lack of use—said yes. Her sisters weren't noted for being shy and retiring, which only made Leila all the more intriguing. And when she turned to look at him with eyes that, apart from being very beautiful, were wide and candid, he registered a most definite physical response.

'Come,' he said, forging a passage for her through the crowd. 'Let's get you sorted out so you can enjoy the party.'

Leila bit her lip to hide her smile. The thought of Raffa Leon 'sorting her out' was rather appealing. Thank goodness she had more sense.

There was one good thing about all this. Everyone was so busy staring at Raffa as they walked through the lobby that no one noticed Leila, or the mud on her clothes.

Shame on you, Leila Skavanga! Wasn't this supposed to be your breakout year?

Pegged as the dreamer of the family—the youngest, the quietest, the peacemaker—if she was ever going to break out of that safe, cosy mould, she had to change, and she had to change now. But not all those changes had to happen tonight. In fact, it would be safer if they didn't. When she had made that promise to herself that she would change, and that she could change, she hadn't factored the devil at her side into the equation. Don Rafael Leon, the Duke of Cantalabria, to give Raffa his full title, was not the sort of man to practise anything on. She had set her heart on finding the modern-day equivalent of a pipe and slippers man— someone undemanding and kind. Someone safe. And Raffa Leon was not safe.

So what about his chivalry towards her?

Innate politeness, she decided. Even great whites had the decency to circle you before they struck.

She exclaimed as Raffa grabbed her hands to draw her in front of him beneath the searching light of one of the hotel's glittering chandeliers.

'*Dios,* Leila! This is worse than I thought!'

Standing back, he stared long and hard at her ruined

clothes, while she was only capable of registering the unaccustomed heat flooding through her.

'Are you sure you didn't hurt yourself?' Raffa demanded.

'No, not at all...' She just wanted to stand there for a moment longer, enjoying the heat and strength in his hands. How cold and limp hers must seem by comparison, she thought, tightening her grip. She quickly released her grip, realising she had given Raffa entirely the wrong message.

'Well, I'm not going to let you out of my sight tonight,' he said with a hint of humour in his eyes as if he knew how awkward she felt having touched him. 'We can't risk any more accidents.'

'Agreed,' she murmured, still staring at him like a loon.

'The restroom, Leila?'

'Of course.' Mentally, she shook herself. 'And, really, I'm fine—I can handle it.'

'Can you?'

'Without you,' she confirmed pleasantly.

So ignore my wishes, she thought as Raffa drew her by the hand across the lobby, where the crowd parted for him like the Red Sea.

'I'm sure you've got places to be, people to meet, Raffa.'

'Yes,' he agreed. 'Right here with you, making sure the rest of your evening goes better than the start has. And you're not keeping me, Leila. Any excuse to avoid a night of small talk with people I don't know, don't want to know and will never see again.' At this point he gave a delicious Latin shrug that drew her gaze to the width of his shoulders. 'Getting away from the crowd is great for me, Leila.'

She'd felt exactly the same when she'd left the house, but only because she was so shy in a crowd of people she didn't know, which surely couldn't be Raffa's problem.

'I've been thinking back to Britt's wedding,' Raffa admitted as they waited their turn in the queue for the cloakroom. 'I remember you playing tag with those tiny flower girls. You did a great job of keeping them entertained.'

'I enjoyed it too,' she admitted. 'I'm afraid sophistication is not my middle name.'

'Some might call it charming, Leila.'

Her secret was out. She loved children. In fact, she loved children and animals more than most adults outside her family, because they were straightforward and she wasn't good at playing mind games.

'Our turn,' Raffa prompted with his hand in the small of her back as the queue to the cloakroom cleared.

His touch lit every part of her with awareness. Maybe because his hand was so strong, and his touch was so light...

'So, you like children?'

'Yes, I do.' Handing his borrowed jacket over, she turned to face the man she was sure would rather be a million miles away and hit back defensively. 'As a matter of fact, I can't wait to have children. I just don't want the man.'

Raffa's lips pressed down in the most attractive way. 'Could be awkward.'

She frowned. 'Why?'

'Biology?'

If there was some sort of danger/beware register, Raffa should be put on it, Leila decided as he flashed his wicked smile.

She had a lucky escape from more verbal jousting

when her gorgeous sister Britt chose that moment to enter the hotel on the arm of her handsome sheikh. Spotting them immediately, Britt gave Leila a what-the-heck-are-you-doing-with-*him?* look, swiftly followed by a jerk of her beautiful blonde head in the direction of the elevators—a signal that Leila should get herself out of trouble and up to the family suite pronto, before she got herself into deeper water with the most dangerous man in town.

She returned Britt's look with a slanting smile that said, do I have to?

Did she want to? That was the question.

Britt shrugged as if to say, on your head be it.

It was all right for Britt. Fantastic in company like Leila's other sister, Eva, Britt would be an asset to any gathering, while Leila would only get in the way if she went up to the suite Britt had taken for her pre-party gathering.

'Put your ticket away safely, Leila.'

'Sorry?'

'Your cloakroom ticket,' Raffa prompted, handing it over. 'Now get yourself into the restroom to sort out your dress. And, okay—' His gaze descended and lingered for quite some time. 'Your stockings are shot.'

'My tights,' she corrected him primly.

'Please don't disillusion me.'

That smile!

Her equilibrium having been taken and turned upside down, it was definitely time to take a short break from the hottest man around. 'Don't bother waiting up for me,' she called over her shoulder with a grin as she headed at speed for the restroom.

She'd given him an out. Hopefully, he'd take the hint. Leaning over the washbasin, she took a much-needed moment to catch her breath. Forget the dress. Forget the mud. Her mind was full of the man outside that door. Would he wait for her? Almost certainly not, thank goodness. No one had ever had this sort of effect on her before. Which had to mean she was certifiably crazy. Raffa Leon had a reputation that made Casanova look like a choirboy. He was single because he played the field. And she had no intention of applying to become a member of his team.

Pulling back from the basin, she tore off a strip of paper towel and, wetting it, cleaned the mud off her dress. The dress was soon okay-ish, but, as Raffa had clearly identified, her tights were ruined. Stripping them off, she dumped them in the bin.

Bare legs?

She pulled a face. Chalk legs weren't exactly the look she'd been aiming for, but who would notice?

Raffa.

Raffa noticed everything.

But he probably wouldn't even speak to her again that night. And if he did, wasn't this year supposed to be about chilling out and freeing herself to do some of the things she had longed to do—like travelling, like meeting new people, for instance? And if he was waiting outside the door for her, why shouldn't she allow him to escort her to the party? Britt and Eva wouldn't miss her up in their suite. They would be heavily into hosting cocktails and canapés by now. And Raffa was surely more entertaining than the mayor of Skavanga, whose unofficial job it was to make a wallflower feel valued. Or the elderly vicar, who could always be relied upon to give Leila a pep talk on finding a husband before it was too late.

Too late at twenty-two?

And who needed a husband, anyway? All she wanted was a child—children, preferably. She was perennially broody. And, in the unlikely event that Raffa was desperate enough to be outside that door, she would be well chaperoned at the party. Britt and Eva would be there with their partners, along with a hundred or so guests. And it wasn't every day she got to swap small talk with a billionaire.

So… Would he be there? Or would Raffa Leon have breathed a sigh of relief the moment she closed the restroom door and made his escape? Before her courage deserted her completely, she opened the door to find out.

'Leila.'

'Raffa…'

So far, so disastrous. One glance into those laughing dark eyes and she could hardly breathe. Raffa looked amazing—even more than amazing. In a dark, formal suit that moulded his powerful body to perfection, he was taller than most of the other men present, and exuded energy like a fighter jet amongst a fleet of biplanes.

'I apologise for keeping you waiting so long.'

'It was worth the wait, Leila. You look sensational.'

What? She stopped just short of rolling her eyes. Then, remembering this was another example of his practised charm, she filed his compliment away under Trivia.

'Well, at least I'm mud free,' she agreed, glancing down at her clothes. Unfortunately, under the lights they still looked a bit ropey. 'I had to take my tights off—'

Uh? What kind of message did that send?

There was laughter in Raffa's eyes, but now she couldn't stop herself and nerves were starting to make her babble. 'Bare legs… Well… White legs, actually—'

Good of you to point it out, she could imagine him thinking.

Great legs, he thought. And the rest was very nicely packaged too. Leila was wearing the same dress she'd worn at Britt's wedding when she had been playing with the children. He remembered it now.

'Britt's dress,' Leila said, seeing him look at it. 'I wore it at my sister's wedding.'

'I remember.' And Leila would win any Who-looks-best-in-this-dress? contest hands down.

'It's the prettiest dress I've ever seen,' she rattled on as if she had to excuse the fact that she was wearing something that suited her so well. 'I begged Britt not to go to the expense of buying some silly bridesmaid's dress I'd never wear again—and, look! Here I am, wearing it again! That's what I call getting your money's worth...'

As Leila's hectic explanation petered out, he hummed, wondering why she didn't have any pretty dresses of her own to wear.

And why should he care?

'It's a bit too tight,' she said, getting her second wind. 'Britt's so slim—'

The tighter the better, as far as he was concerned. He'd never gone for the half-starved look. The dress would always look better on Leila because she was voluptuous.

'I don't go to many parties. Don't feel sorry for me,' she insisted before he had chance to say a word. 'I usually hang out somewhere quieter than this—'

'My preference too,' he said, shielding Leila with his arm as more guests piled into the lobby. Quiet rooms and hot women would be his preference every time. 'Here's an idea—' He had stopped in front of the eleva-

tor. 'There's a quiet lounge just down this corridor. Why
don't we take five? It would give you chance to recover
your composure.' And calm down a bit, he thought.

'You mean, I look a mess?'

She looked adorable and so trusting as she turned
her face up to his. Well, she was safe tonight. He had
already reined in his thoughts from champagne and se-
duction to soft drinks and a few very necessary moments
of calm for Leila. She needed to relax before facing the
bright lights of the party, and, surprising even himself,
he wanted to get to know her a little better. 'Come on—
let's get out of this crush. The party isn't due to start for
another half hour,' he reassured her when she looked
doubtful. 'We won't be missed.'

'But my sisters are expecting me.'

'Your sisters will be so busy doing what they do well,
they won't miss either of us.'

Opening the door on the tempting setting of a quiet
lounge, he stood back. They wouldn't be alone. There
were quite a few residents who weren't going to the party
sitting around reading newspapers and chatting quietly,
and there was a big, welcoming log fire burning lustily
in the grate. There were still plenty of cosy armchairs
where they could sit and chat without being overheard.
It was the perfect spot for a girl who wasn't sure of herself yet, or of her companion.

'This is lovely,' Leila said with relief, gazing round.

'Orange juice?' he suggested.

'With a splash of lemonade, please. How did you
know?'

He loved the way Leila's smile lit up her face. 'Lucky
guess.' Not such a stretch. It was going to be a long
night, and, though Leila was reputedly the shyest of
the Skavanga sisters, there was a hint of steel about her

that suggested she would face the party clear-headed or not at all.

Leila intrigued him, if only because she was so different from her sisters. The middle sister, Eva, whose eve-of-wedding party this was, could be a headstrong handful, while Britt was a hard-nosed businesswoman who only softened for her sheikh. Leila's sisters and her brother, Tyr, had clearly protected her when their parents died, as Leila had been so very young when the tragic planc crash happened, but the intuition that had never let him down so far said there was more to Leila Skavanga than simply a sheltered girl who worked in the archive department of the Skavanga mining museum, and he was keen to find out what that was.

CHAPTER TWO

WHAT EXACTLY WAS she doing with Raffa Leon? What could they possibly have to talk about?

Anybody?

She had never done anything so out of character in her life. Yes, Raffa was charming, but he was practically a stranger—and a dangerous one at that, according to her sisters and the rather more scandalous tone of the press. Leila had always been glad she worked in a separate building from the mining company, if only because it put some space between herself and these high-powered, fast-living types.

But didn't this unexpected encounter with a leading player in the consortium dovetail nicely with her determination to make this her breakout year?

Roar mouse?

Great idea, if she had the courage to summon up something more than a squeak. And what was Raffa up to? Why choose to spend time with her?

'Shall we sit here?' he suggested, indicating two comfortable armchairs facing each other across a sleek glass table.

'Thank you.'

Even this close to such a powerhouse of testosterone made her feel incredibly aware and wary. His deep, velvety voice with that intriguing accent played in her head, and she had to remind herself that sweeping a woman away with whatever means he chose to employ was Raffa Leon's stock in trade. Though he was hardly out to seduce her with so many other attractive women at the party.

Out of the archive department into the fire, she concluded with amusement as Raffa turned to give their order to the waiter. He looked so relaxed, while she was more like a schoolgirl on parade, sitting stiff and upright in her chair, waiting for the pronouncements of the headmaster.

Raffa knocked that idea on its head the moment he turned back to her. No headmaster on earth looked like this—such compelling dark eyes with that touch of humour, and a wickedly curving mouth.

'I'm looking forward to a refreshing drink, without having it knocked out of our hands,' he said, turning up the voltage on his smile.

It took her a moment to speak, she was so captivated, and then she experienced a moment of panic. What could she possibly say to him? How did you launch into a conversation with a notorious billionaire? How's your yacht? Would that do?

'What are you smiling at, Leila?' he enquired, raising one sweeping ebony brow in a way that made her heart stop.

'Am I smiling?' She stopped smiling immediately. 'I was just thinking, this is a great place, isn't it? Such a good idea of yours.' She made a point of staring round. Anything was safer than looking at Raffa.

'It's good to see you relax,' he said, his eyes dark like the night and just as full of danger.

Relaxed? Was that what he thought? She doubted

any woman could relax around Raffa Leon. He had this way of staring directly into your eyes that made it hard to look away. Impossible to look away, she amended.

So come out of your shell. Live boldly for once.

'Here's your juice,' he said. 'With a splash of lemonade as requested.'

As he handed it to her he was doing that eye thing—the curving smile, the crinkle at the corner of his eyes. It was all too easy to fool herself into thinking he was interested in her, when this was just his way. Raffa Leon was a charming and accomplished seducer, both in business and with women, and she had to get it into her head that this was just an innocent encounter and a refreshing drink. She had never been the type of girl men took up to their room. She was the kid sister they brought into the very public hotel lounge to share an orange juice with before the party.

And she should be pleased about that.

She *was* pleased. But she would be lying if she tried to pretend it wouldn't be thrilling to have Raffa look at her with something other than humour in his eyes.

When she leaned forward to pick up her glass, her senses filled with the faint scent of his cologne. It was one of those intoxicating scents, hard to identify, but undoubtedly exclusive. She sat back again, wondering. What now? Raffa seemed content to let the silence hang between them, so maybe it was up to her to break the silence. Live boldly, for once! Pointing through one of the tall arched windows, she drew his attention to the park, picked out in lights at this time of night. 'My mother used to take me over there to the park when I was a little girl so I could terrorise people on my three-wheeler.'

'I never saw you as a hoodlum, Leila.'

So how did he see her? Raffa laughed as he set down his drink. A soft drink too, she noted.

Raffa felt his heart stir as he thought about a little girl taking every day with her mother for granted, and a young mother enjoying special time with her youngest child. Those days must have felt as if they would go on for ever. Neither of them could have anticipated Leila's father's descent into drunken violence, or the tragic plane crash and loss of life.

'What are you thinking about now?' he prompted, though he guessed Leila had inadvertently uncovered memories she didn't normally share with strangers, and was probably regretting being so open with him. Insanely, he wanted to hug her and tell her it would be all right, but they didn't know each other well enough for that. They had a party to go to, where Leila would have to be bright and cheerful, or her sisters would want to know why. He didn't want to leave her shakier than when she'd fallen into his arms outside the hotel. What had begun as basic attraction and curiosity had gained an edge of care. Not that he felt responsible for Leila, and she wouldn't want that. She'd been doing pretty well on her own up to now.

'More juice?'

'Please. Sorry, Raffa, I was miles away.'

Thinking about her mother's letter, Leila realised as Raffa turned away to order more drinks. She'd been doing a lot of that recently, and she'd had plenty of time to memorise every word over the years.

My darling Leila,
I love you more than life itself, and want you to
promise me that you will live your life to the full.
You're only a little girl now, but one day you'll be

a woman with choices to make and I want you to
make the right choices.

Don't be afraid of life, Leila, as I have been. Be
bold in all you do—

It still haunted her to think her mother must have
known she was in danger—maybe even that Leila's father would go too far and kill them both. Leila had been
too young to understand what had happened at the time
of the crash, and it was only later when she was older
that her sisters had explained that their father was most
likely drunk at the controls of the plane. She'd done
some investigating of her own at the local newspaper
office and had got the picture of a violent alcoholic and
a woman who had been the helpless victim of his rages.

'Ice in your juice?' Raffa broke into her thoughts.

'No. It's delicious as it is, thank you.'

'Spanish oranges,' he said, his dark face brightening
with a smile. 'The best.'

'You're partial.'

'Yes, I am,' he agreed, holding her gaze a beat too
long.

It was long enough for her heart to pound out of control. Raffa was so worldly, and it was almost funny, the
two of them being here together, when Skavanga was
just one stop on Raffa's round-the-world tour of his in-
ternational business interests, and she had never been
outside the town except for university, and even then
she'd only gone a few miles down the road to the local
college. As soon as she had qualified, she'd scuttled
back to the place she knew best, the place she felt safest,
where she could hide away in the archive department of
a mining museum where it was quiet, and where there

was no chance of meeting a wife beater, or an alcoholic. Or anyone for that matter.

'So you've stayed in Skavanga all your life, Leila? Leila?' Raffa prompted, his voice shaking her round.

She'd been trapped in the past, sitting on the stairs, listening to her parents arguing and hearing the inevitable thump when her mother hit the floor. And now, judging by the concerned look on Raffa's face, he was joining her on this trip down memory lane too.

'Yes, I've been here all my life,' she confirmed brightly to make up for her lapse in concentration.

She was actually quite good at being jolly. She'd had plenty of practice over the years. Having been totally eclipsed by her beautiful sisters, she'd had the choice of being the mouse in the background, or the jolly sister. She'd perfected both. 'I've always been close to my brother and sisters.' At least, she had been, until her brother, Tyr, had gone missing.

'It's great to have siblings,' Raffa agreed, 'even if you don't always get along.'

'We get along. I just miss my brother, and I wish I knew where he was.' Her stare met Raffa's, but, if he knew where Tyr was, he wasn't telling. 'I know it must look to you as if my sisters run roughshod over me, but believe me, Raffa, I can hold my own.'

'I never doubted it,' he agreed, to her surprise.

But as Raffa's smile faded, and a shadow crossed his face, she wondered about his family. She also realised they had relaxed into the last thing she had imagined sharing with Raffa Leon, which was a meaningful conversation.

'What about you?' she prompted gently. 'What about your family, Raffa?'

The look he shot her made her regret asking. 'I'm sorry. I didn't mean to probe.'

'That's all right,' he said, sitting back. He shrugged. 'Apart from the three brothers and two sisters I do know about, I'm told I have countless half brothers and sisters across the globe, thanks to the untiring efforts of my father.'

'And your mother—?' That was one question she definitely shouldn't have asked, Leila realised, breaking off when she saw the expression on Raffa's face. 'I'm sorry. I—'

'Don't be,' he interrupted. 'I was lucky enough to spend most of my youth with my grandmother. As soon as my elder brothers and sisters went off to college, my father made it quite clear that he was done with children.'

'So there was no place at home for you?'

He didn't answer that. He didn't need to. What Raffa had told her explained so much about him. He was the lone wolf, dangerous, hidden and unknowable.

'I'd like to meet your grandmother,' she said, trying to bring him back to the present. 'She must be an amazing woman.'

'To take me on?' Raffa queried, relaxing into a laugh. 'She is. And maybe you will meet her one day, Leila.'

He was just being polite, but it was a relief to see him smiling again.

'And you grew up with your sisters and brother,' he prompted.

'Who always teased me unmercifully,' she confirmed.

'And you don't mind that?'

'I tease them back. Families,' she added with a smile and a shrug.

Raffa huffed softly and smiled back at her.

His eyes were so incredibly expressive they warmed

her right through. The fact that Raffa was as hot as hell should have been warning enough for her to back off, but he was like a magnet drawing her closer, against her will. 'My sisters tease me because they love me as much as I love them,' she said to break the sudden electric tension between them. 'I guess they're always trying to make up for—'

'Your mother dying when you were so very young,' Raffa cut in.

The concern on his face surprised her. 'I suppose… Anyway, they've been great.' Massive understatement. 'Tyr too—' She stopped as the familiar ache washed over her.

'Your brother will come home one day soon, Leila.'

'You say that with such certainty. Have you heard from Tyr?' There was excitement in her voice, but Raffa disappointed her by saying nothing. And why was she surprised? Leila and her sisters had always suspected that the three men in the consortium knew exactly where Tyr was, but none of them would reveal his whereabouts. The four men had been at school together, and then again in Special Forces, so their loyalties cut deep. But still, she had to try. 'All I care about is that he's safe, Raffa.'

Her heart lurched as she stared deep into eyes that held her gaze steadily.

'Please don't ask me questions about your brother, Leila, because I can't tell you the answers you want to hear.'

'You won't tell me,' she argued.

'That's right,' Raffa agreed levelly. 'I won't.'

'But perhaps you could tell me he's safe?'

There was a long pause, and then Raffa said, 'He's safe.'

'Thank you.' Relief flooded through her as she sat

back. Tyr was safe. That was all she needed to hear, and the thought that Raffa knew her brother so well made everything she'd heard about him pale into insignificance.

'Tell me about your job at the museum, Leila.'

She relaxed. There was nothing she loved more than talking about her job. She enjoyed working at the museum so much she could talk about it endlessly. 'It's my passion—' She didn't need to try now. The words just came pouring out. 'I'd love to show you round. It's amazing. I wish you could see all the things we've found. To think my ancestors used them. And every day there's a new discovery...' She stopped in case she was boring him, but Raffa encouraged her to go on. And so it all came pouring out—her plans for the museum, her hopes and dreams for the future of the work she loved, her classes, her workshops, her tours, the exhibitions she had planned.

'I am so sorry,' she said at last. 'I must have bored the socks off you. No one can stop me once I get talking about the museum.'

'On the contrary, I don't want to stop you,' he insisted, 'though it is a revelation to discover you're not the quiet sister after all.'

'I'm not quiet at all,' she assured him.

No. Leila just needed the chance to be heard, he thought.

'What are you doing?' she said when he took the glass from her hand.

'I think we should go to the party. Have you seen the time?'

'No. Goodness me!' she exclaimed, springing up. 'I have been boring you!'

'Not at all,' he insisted. 'Far from it. This evening has

turned out far better than I anticipated, and we haven't even reached the party yet.'

We?

She laughed as Raffa smiled back at her. Even if he was just being polite, she was having a great time. Raffa Leon was so much more than she had expected in every way. It was hard not to be attracted to him—impossible. Which was in itself crazy. Who invited trouble, unless they were completely mad?

She did, apparently.

'So, are you completely recovered after your tumble?' he said as he escorted her across the crowded lobby.

'Completely,' she confirmed. 'And thank you for the drink. I feel ready for anything now.'

When Raffa laughed at this, she realised he must think her quaint and old-fashioned; sheltered, certainly.

'If I were as honest as you, Leila, I would never have succeeded in business,' he confided to her obvious alarm. 'Meaning everything shows on your face,' he was quick to explain when she frowned. 'I'm not quite the big bad wolf I'm reported to be.'

'But close.' She laughed.

He laughed too. It was good to see Leila relaxed. And he wanted her to know he did have principles. He didn't want her fretting about some rogue buying into her family business. Leila had certainly brought out the best in him. And that was a first.

'And now to find your sisters,' he said, realising that with any other attractive woman, finding her sisters would be the last thing on his mind.

'Must we?'

Leila had spoken without thinking, he realised as her cheeks flushed red. She was enjoying being relaxed.

She'd never been keen to join the pre-party scrum in Britt's suite.

'We don't have to go up to Britt's suite,' he reassured her. 'We can meet your sisters in the ballroom at our table. I'm looking forward to seeing the three of you together. Life is never boring with a Skavanga sister, so they tell me.'

'They're right,' Leila admitted wryly. 'Just your bad luck you got landed with me.'

'Am I complaining?'

She flashed him a mischievous look, and as her mouth curved in a smile Leila's eyes lit in a way that made him want to know more about this youngest Skavanga sister. It hit him out of nowhere that his grandmother would love her. His *abuelita,* as cute little grannies were known in Spain, was never off his case, always insisting he must find himself a *good* woman. He would do a lot of things for Abuelita, but not that, though his grandmother would put the bunting out if he brought a girl like Leila home.

And hadn't Leila said she wanted to meet his grandmother?

He glanced at her, thinking the best thing about Leila was she had no idea how attractive she was, and in his world that was definitely a breath of fresh air.

They were halfway across the ballroom when she got a call on her phone. 'Britt,' she mouthed. As she pressed the receiver to her ear her cheeks turned scarlet. He gathered she wasn't having the easiest of conversations with her sister.

'She wanted to know where I was,' Leila explained when she ended the call.

'I hope you told her, living dangerously?'

'With the big bad wolf? Yes, I did, as it happens.'

'And your sister hit the roof?'

'Pretty much.'

They shared an amused look.

'Do you believe everything you've heard about me, Leila?'

For a moment she didn't speak, but then she said quite bluntly, 'I don't know you well enough to pass judgement yet.'

He laughed at that. 'When you do—you will let me know?'

'I'll make sure of it.'

She hadn't told Raffa the whole truth about her conversation with Britt, who was clearly worried about her, and who had yelled in alarm at the prospect of her baby sister spending even one minute alone in the company of the notorious Raffa Leon. Worse luck, Raffa had turned out to be the perfect gentleman, though it might be fun to tease her sisters. It wasn't often Leila caused comment.

'You did reassure Britt?' Raffa commented as they approached the table.

'Actually, no,' she admitted. 'For once in my life, I was enigmatic. I was only having a bit of fun, but I couldn't resist it. My sisters tease me constantly, so this was my chance to get them back.'

'Well, I'm happy to go along with however you want to play it,' Raffa assured her, his dark eyes glinting in a way that filled her mind with all sorts of outrageous possibilities.

'I might take you up on that.'

'Please do.'

His smile could travel to places she had forgotten about, in no time flat. 'Then I will,' she added with a smile and a shrug, thinking this evening was going to be fun.

'Tonight will see Leila Skavanga come to the fore,' Raffa promised as he held her chair.

'But I don't want to upset them,' Leila was quick to add. 'Britt has gone to a lot of trouble to arrange the party for Eva, and I don't want anything to spoil Eva's night.'

'I promise you, it won't,' Raffa agreed, 'not through anything I do, anyway, though there's nothing to prevent us having a bit of fun. I just hope with all the Skavanga Diamonds glittering at once you don't dazzle me into a stupor.'

'No chance of that,' Leila said, laughing at Raffa's expression as she sat down.

Warmth flooded her as Raffa sat down in the next chair, close but not too close, almost touching but not touching, in a way that made her thighs tingle.

'You can rely on me to back you up with enough smouldering looks and dirty dancing to shock your sisters out of their killer shoes.'

'Wonderful.' Did she mean to say that? Yes, she did. 'That should make my home life a whole lot easier,' she commented dryly.

'Any time I can be of service...'

And this was a really bad time to be holding Raffa's stare. His eyes were dancing with laughter, which told her nothing about his thoughts, but if this connection between them was only for tonight, it was the most fun she'd had in a long time. And now Britt and Eva had arrived in the ballroom on the arms of their handsome partners, bringing an end to their conversation as every head in the ballroom swivelled round.

'Don't look so worried, Leila,' Raffa murmured, leaning in close. 'I promise not to do anything that might upset them.'

Once she stared at Raffa it was hard to look away. 'Something tells me Eva and Britt aren't going to believe we've been sitting, chatting in the lounge all this time.'

And the truth was even more complicated than that, Leila realised. Both of them had touched on subjects she guessed neither of them would dream of discussing with a stranger, and the connection she'd sensed between them at first had grown stronger because of it.

'You'll just have to put up with your sisters' suspicions,' Raffa said pragmatically, leaning back as he prepared to stand to greet their dinner companions.

'Just so long as we don't take this too far,' Leila agreed, already wondering what she'd got herself into as Raffa turned to bestow a lingering look on her face.

'You and I know what went on.'

Precisely nothing, she thought as the most handsome man in the room went on to list their harmless pastimes. 'You drank juice. We talked. We relaxed. But there's no way on earth your sisters are going to believe that, so unless you'd rather pretend we haven't been together every second since you arrived at the hotel—'

'You make our innocent time together sound so bad.'

'What fun would it be otherwise?' he murmured.

She hummed as Raffa's black gaze bored deep into hers.

'Let the teasing begin,' he said.

Had it already? she wondered as Raffa leaned in close. And was she the main target? If Britt and Eva had been suspicious before, seeing the two of them like this, so close they were practically kissing, would turn her sisters into tireless seekers after the truth. But she hadn't done anything wrong. She was following the advice in her mother's letter and being bold.

And even when Raffa smiled his slow, sexy smile, she asked herself, was it likely Britt and Eva would imagine she'd had hot monkey sex with Raffa Leon?

Absolutely not!

So what did she have to worry about?

She could relax.

Britt and Eva stared first at Raffa, and then at their sister. 'Well,' Britt said, smiling as they greeted her. 'Here you are, Leila.' She exchanged an arch-browed look with Eva.

'I'm really sorry we missed the reception upstairs,' Leila began, slipping easily back into the role of peacemaker, 'but—'

'But we got talking,' Raffa intervened smoothly.

'I'm sure you did,' Eva agreed dryly.

'We were in the lounge,' Leila chipped in.

'Of course you were,' Britt agreed.

Raffa was right. They were never going to believe her. She glanced at him, only for Raffa to give her an amused and conspiratorial look. Let the teasing begin, he'd said. But let's not overdo it, her eyes begged him as her sisters sat down. This was Eva's special night, and she didn't want anything to spoil it.

Raffa returned her look with a reassuring expression. She'd never had a co-conspirator before. And it was quite incredible to think she belonged with such a party of swans, Leila mused as everyone started talking at once. Eva looked off-the-scale stunning, with her long, flame-red hair caught back on either side of her beautiful face with glittering diamond combs, her fabulous figure displayed in a floor-length, body-hugging gown of flesh-coloured lace, embellished with tiny crystals. And the heat flying between Eva and Count Roman Quisvada, the man she would marry tomorrow, was off the scale.

Would a man ever look at her that way? Leila wondered as she turned her attention to Britt, whose husband, Sheikh Sharif, was currently shooting intensely personal messages into his wife's eyes. With her icy

Nordic looks, imposing height and slender figure, Britt was the perfect foil for her Arabian prince, and there was such closeness between them, Leila couldn't help but feel wistful.

There was such an overload of glamour at their table they were the focus of the room. Three amazing-looking men, two fabulous-looking women…and Leila. Her sisters set a standard she couldn't hope to compete with, but for one night, with Raffa at her side, she was going to give it a shot.

'Would you like me to help you choose from the menu, Leila?' Raffa murmured, leaning in close.

Britt and Eva were instantly on alert, but she felt obliged to point out, 'It's a fixed menu.'

'So it is,' Raffa agreed, not losing eye contact with her for a moment.

It was going to be hard remembering this was just pretence, but a glance at her sisters reassured her they were convinced.

'Would you like me to read the menu out to you?' Raffa now suggested.

'Yes, please,' she said, sitting back with the air of a woman for whom men peeled grapes.

Britt and Eva had designed the menu between them and Leila soon realised that her sisters had chosen food which was impossible to eat without appearing provocative—a look Leila was keen to avoid tonight, even if her intention was to tease them, as she had to balance the game with not taking things too far with Raffa.

The appetiser was a small baked cheese drizzled with truffle oil on a bed of salad leaves…

'Don't you like cheese, Leila?'

As Raffa asked the question Britt and Eva stared at her. She loved cheese and they knew it. Britt had probably designed this first course with Leila's preferences in mind. But the thought of all that soft, warm cheese glistening on her lips—

'Shall we swap plates?' Raffa suggested.

She lifted the plate. He reached for it, and their fingers touched. Heat exploded inside her. Her gasp could probably be heard in the car park.

'I love a man with a healthy appetite,' Britt commented, flashing a look at Eva.

'What's the matter, baby sister?' Eva contributed, picking up the virtual ball Britt had just lobbed across the net. 'Not enough hot food for you around this table?'

'I've got an enormous appetite,' Raffa confessed with every appearance of innocence. 'If any of you don't want your food, please pass it my way.'

The other men registered small smiles at this, while Britt and Eva exchanged a knowing look.

Okay. She got it. Leila was Little Red Riding Hood paired with the big bad wolf for the night. She gave her sisters a warning look, but they just smiled and raised a brow. As long as she could handle it, they were okay with it. Now she just had to watch out that the joke didn't end up on her.

The next course was asparagus, which was possibly Leila's favourite food, but the way Eva was sucking the butter off the tip...

'I can't believe you're not eating this,' Raffa scolded when she again offered to exchange her plate with him, but his eyes were laughing, as if he knew exactly what she was thinking.

'I don't want to risk butter dripping down my dress.' She raised a brow at him, conscious that her sisters were watching them closely. 'This dress has been through enough adventures for one night, don't you agree, Raffa?'

As Britt and Eva exchanged a look, Leila appeared to change her mind, and, lifting a buttery spear to her lips, she sucked on it thoughtfully.

'Here—have another one if you're hungry,' he prompted in a way that made her breath catch.

Her sisters were transfixed by now, while the look in Raffa's eyes wasn't doing all that much for her own equilibrium. It was just an act, she told herself, until he captured some butter from her lips on his thumb and sucked it clean. She felt an answering pulse of pleasure with each lazy tug of his mouth. It was such a sexy, intimate thing for him to do.

And she should look away.

When it came to the entrée, a black pepper filet mignon with a blob of Gorgonzola on top, resting on a bed of wilted spinach, she was still watching Raffa eat.

'Hmm, delicious,' he murmured, savouring the delicious meat. 'Why aren't you eating, Leila?'

'It's chocolate fondue for pudding,' Britt remarked innocently.

Okay, there was no leaving this game half played. 'Chocolate fondue?' She gazed deep into Raffa's eyes. 'My favourite…'

As Raffa paused, fork suspended, she tucked in with relish. This was easy. Where had she been hiding all these years?

'Leila.'

Why was Raffa whispering?

She turned to look at him with confidence. 'Yes? What is it? What's wrong?'

She prickled with awareness as he leaned in close.

'You've got spinach between your teeth…'

CHAPTER THREE

IT WAS INEVITABLE the conversation around the table would eventually return to the hottest topic of the night: where had Leila and Raffa been for such a long time? Britt and Eva clearly weren't convinced by the hotel lounge story.

'So, what did you two find to talk about up in Raffa's suite?' Britt asked casually.

'We weren't in Raffa's suite,' Leila said patiently. 'We were chatting in the hotel lounge, surrounded by other guests—' She was just getting into her stride when her eyes widened with surprise as Raffa's warm, strong hand covered hers in a cautionary gesture.

'We were discussing the mining museum, as a matter of fact,' he commented casually. 'Leila's got some great ideas,' he went on without missing a beat. 'And I was saying that, as I have one of the finest gem collections in the world, perhaps Leila should visit my island with a view to displaying a selection of her choice in Skavanga.'

The silence was absolute. Everyone was stunned, including Leila. Raffa had just hit them with the conversation stopper of all time. Was that a serious invitation? Or was he still playing games?

'Just say yes,' he suggested, easing back on his chair as she looked at him.

For once, Britt had nothing to say, and it was Eva who filled the gap in her usual blunt manner. 'What are you suggesting?' she asked Raffa suspiciously, flying in defence of her sister.

'I'm suggesting Leila comes to Isla Montaña de Fuego to take a look at my jewels,' Raffa responded quietly.

'Why?' Eva was keen to dig deeper before she let him off the hook. 'Why does Leila need to visit your island? Can't you bring the gems here?'

'I wouldn't presume to make a selection for Leila,' Raffa explained smoothly, his black stare confirming this with Leila.

'That's right.' Leila's heart was going crazy as she played along. 'I can't wait to see Raffa's collection. Everyone loves a big diamond, don't they, Eva?'

Britt and Eva quickly hid their ring hands under the table as Raffa added, 'Leila sees a great future for the mining museum.'

'You two have been chatting, haven't you?' Eva commented, relaxing back, defeated for once.

As her sisters exchanged a look Leila wondered how long she could keep this up. Visiting Raffa's island? As if! 'Yes, Raffa and I have been talking,' she confirmed blithely. 'It's only natural when we've got so much in common— The diamonds,' she added when her sisters stared at her in disbelief.

'Indeed,' Eva murmured with amusement. 'The diamonds. I'd almost forgotten them.'

'Well, I can't think of any other reason I'd visit the island—' As she spoke Leila was conscious of digging an even bigger hole for herself, but somehow she couldn't stop. 'As soon as I slipped on the ice and Raffa caught me, I thought—what luck! This is my chance to put my business proposition to him—'

'Your what?' Britt interrupted.

Fair enough. She'd gone too far. When were Leila Skavanga and business ever mentioned in the same sentence? Try never.

'Leila made a very good pitch, actually,' Raffa said, filling the gap. 'Water, anyone? Sparkling…? Still…?'

'Leila *is* brilliant at her job,' Britt mused out loud as if she was actually convinced.

'And has always seen her work as an opportunity to give a whole new generation an insight into the business that put the town on the map,' Eva added, shooting a proud-sister look at Leila.

Oh, no! Why were her sisters getting involved? She felt really bad now. If only they would stop being so helpful! Didn't they realise this was all a joke? It so obviously was—

She looked at Raffa, who was giving nothing away. But why pretend to invite her to his island? That was going a bit far, wasn't it?

She almost jumped out of her skin when he reached across to give her hand a reassuring squeeze, and realised she had to say something quickly to Britt and Eva or they would be completely sucked in. 'He's only joking about the trip—even Raffa couldn't be such a glutton for punishment as to invite me to spend more time with him.' She shared an amused look with Britt and Eva and saw them relax.

'Well, the invitation's on the table, Leila.'

Her head shot round to Raffa. *What?* 'An hour chatting with me isn't punishment enough?' she pressed, laughing to try and get him out of his predicament.

No dice. And she got the distinct impression her sisters were holding their breath.

'Not nearly long enough,' Raffa said. 'And in case

you're in any doubt,' he added, saying this to everyone around the table, 'I never joke where business is concerned.'

Britt and Eva were transfixed, while Leila's heart was pumping like crazy. If this was a serious offer, and it certainly seemed to be, it would be her first proper trip out of Skavanga. And with Raffa!

As the spotlight swung away and the conversation returned to less controversial topics Raffa's attention remained fixed on her face, leaving her to wonder if she'd survived this game of teasing, or if she was heading for a fall.

'We're going to dance,' Britt announced. 'Leila?'

'Oh, no. I'm okay, thank you.'

'Will you excuse us if we leave you two alone?' Britt pressed, still obviously concerned for Leila.

'Yes, of course,' Leila reassured her. 'You go right ahead.'

Raffa stood politely as both her sisters left the table with their partners, and then he sat down again, while Leila clung to a life raft in the shape of a chair.

'Shall we?' he suggested, glancing at the packed dance floor.

'You want to dance with me?'

'I don't see anyone else sitting here.'

As a smile curved Raffa's lips she knew this was not remotely sensible. 'Dancing's really not my thing.'

'But I thought we had a pact?'

To tease her sisters, not to bring disaster in the shape of a hot, bad man crashing down on her head. 'Don't worry. I won't hold you to our pact.'

'What if I want you to?'

As a catalogue of potential pitfalls flashed through

her head she felt it was time to come clean. 'Really—there's no need to continue being polite to me.'

'Who said I'm being polite?' Raffa demanded, reaching for her hand.

She couldn't refuse—not with people staring at them and shooting admiring glances at Raffa. She stood and exhaled shakily as he drew her by the hand towards the dance floor, and gave another shaky exclamation when he pressed her close. He hadn't been joking about dirty dancing. She could hardly breathe. Or maybe that was too much excitement. Heat was rampaging through her as she came into contact with every alarming contour of his body.

'I thought you wanted to dance,' Raffa prompted when she remained quite still.

'*You* wanted to dance,' she reminded him, reluctant to end her sensory exploration of a man who was every bit as hard as he looked.

'Yes. With you,' he confirmed, tightening his grip.

Raffa didn't take no for an answer, Leila discovered as he swept her round the floor.

And her sisters were watching. Watching? They were agog. And now they were dancing round her to take a closer look. 'Bandits at twelve o'clock,' she warned, making the mistake of meeting the slumbering sexual heat in Raffa's eyes.

'I like your style, Leila Skavanga,' he murmured, his voice all husky and rough.

'Really?' She prepared herself for some glowing compliment from the master of charm. 'Why?'

'Stubborn. Tricky. Unpredictable.' Raffa shrugged. 'I never know what to expect from you.'

Then he wouldn't be surprised when her stiletto hit his foot.

'What's wrong now, Leila?'

She sniffed. 'I'm waiting for the right beat of the music.'

'Ah, a perfectionist.'

'No. A novice.'

'A novice?' Raffa's warm breath brushed her ear. 'I could soon change that.'

Her sharp intake of breath could probably be heard outside the hotel. 'Practice makes perfect.'

'Another topic on which we agree. Have you got the beat yet, Leila?'

She'd got something!

How could they move so well together when they were a complete mismatch? Fire and ice. Raffa's great size compared to her— Well, truthfully, she wasn't exactly small, but she was a lot smaller than he was. But as the music wove its spell and she began to relax she started to enjoy herself, so that by the time they danced past her sisters there was mischief in her blood. She had always been content to stay beneath the radar, allowing Britt and Eva to slug it out, but not tonight. Not with Raffa. So as they danced past her sisters, instead of shrinking into the woodwork, she threw back her hair and sighed, leaving Britt and Eva in no doubt that she wouldn't have dusty archives on her mind tonight.

'Do you know? I think we've done our duty—'

Leila gasped as Raffa took her hand to lead her off the dance floor.

'I'm ready to leave,' he explained as he forged a passage for them through the milling crowd.

Oh, he was? 'But the party's just getting started,' she pointed out, hanging back.

'Haven't you had enough? I know I have…'

She could see the cabs lined up outside the hotel

through one of the windows. Raffa wasn't talking about the party, she realised, cursing herself for being such a dope. He'd had enough of her. She'd get her coat from the cloakroom, he would put her in one of the cabs and she'd be drinking cocoa before you knew it.

'We'll grab our coats before we go up,' he said as they headed for the door.

'Go up where?'

'To my suite,' Raffa said, frowning as if that were obvious.

'Your suite?' She sounded like a parrot now, which was hardly surprising when his suggestion had turned her brain to mush.

'We need to talk,' he said, 'about the project for the museum? Your visit to the island to choose the gems, Leila?' he prompted. 'There are a lot of details we need to sort out before I leave Skavanga after the wedding tomorrow.'

'But I thought that was—' A joke, she had been about to add when Raffa turned away to speak to the cloakroom attendant.

'Ticket, Leila.' He held out his hand as she fumbled in her bag.

So Raffa was serious about her visiting his island. Her throat dried at the thought of working with the man at her side. She wasn't worried about the business side of things—she knew her stuff. But where anything else was concerned...

There wasn't going to be *anything else,* Leila reassured herself as Raffa handed over her jacket. And this opportunity to inspect his famous gem collection was too good to miss. If Raffa would allow her to display some of his world-famous pieces, it would really put Skavanga on the map.

'Ready, Leila?'

'Ready,' she confirmed.

This was her breakout year after all, she consoled herself as they walked towards the bank of elevators. And she was good at her job. What did she have to worry about? This was an amazing opportunity and she should seize it with both hands.

Let the mouse roar?

Yes. But couldn't she have started at a lower volume with a milder man?

It was too late to turn back now. Raffa was already swiping his card for the penthouse floor. 'After you,' he said as the doors slid open.

There couldn't be anything more to this invitation, could there?

Almost certainly not, but as she stared into the small steel cabin she got the sense that once she stepped inside her fate was sealed.

So go back home. Drink cocoa for the rest of your life. Resume mouse duties.

She chose to be bold.

CHAPTER FOUR

LEILA SPENT MOST of the journey up to his suite rattling off her credentials, perhaps because she needed to reassure herself that her degree in Gemology and Business Studies was the only thing that could possibly interest him. She kept this going until the elevator slowed and he pulled away from the wall where he'd been leaning.

'Very interesting,' he assured her. 'But the fact that you played hockey for the university team, and have Grade Eight piano with Distinction, isn't really relevant to me.'

'What is?'

For a moment there was something in his eyes that really, *really* made Leila wish she hadn't asked that question. But then the look was gone, leaving her wondering if she'd imagined it, as Raffa returned to being the soigné billionaire with the slanting smile that could conquer the world.

'Your enthusiasm, Leila,' he explained. 'Your enthusiasm when you talk about the mining museum. Your plans for it, and your dedication to the work you're doing there—with the children especially. You impressed me.'

'Are you saying you were giving me a job interview all the time we were sitting in the lounge?'

'You could put it that way.'

'I see.' Raffa's job offer was no joke, she realised as her heart began to pound.

'I'll square it with Britt,' he added as she frowned in thought. 'I'm sure your sister can get someone to cover for you while you're away.'

Leila smiled at that suggestion. 'I'll square it with Britt. She is my sister, Raffa.' And would have plenty to say about this plan, Leila was sure. 'I should get word to Britt now, in fact, to let her know where I am.'

'You don't have to tell her everything tonight. I recommend choosing another time. You don't want to spoil her party, do you, Leila?'

Raffa's eyes were dark and enigmatic as he held her gaze. 'You can't talk business tonight—or tomorrow at your sister's wedding, for that matter,' he pointed out.

'You're right.' But she also knew her sisters would be discussing her right now. *Does Leila have any idea what she's getting herself into?* she could imagine them saying as she left the ballroom. *Should we rescue her or let her stew?* For the first time in their lives, she guessed Britt and Eva wouldn't have a clue what to do for the best.

'Hey,' Raffa murmured when she frowned. 'Let your sisters sort themselves out for once.'

No one had ever seen her as the pivot of the family before. Leila Skavanga, hub of calm, around which the whirlwind that was Britt and Eva spun?

'What are you smiling at?'

'Your comment about my sisters needing me to sort them out.'

'Well, don't they?'

'Not all the time—'

'All the time, I would say.'

Raffa didn't give her chance to argue. She drew in a shocked breath as he dipped his head to brush her lips with his. It was such a gentle kiss it disarmed her completely. The thought of such a big, brutal-looking man being able to kiss like that was beguiling to the point where she had to tell him. 'You're not supposed to kiss like that.'

'How am I supposed to kiss?'

Heat flashed through her veins as Raffa demonstrated another, more insistent variation on a theme that sucked the breath from her lungs. It wasn't a case of when she roared now, but only how loud.

The elevator slowing to a halt broke them apart, giving her a moment to compose herself before the doors peeled back on a brightly lit Scandi-style corridor.

'We need to get into that detail fast,' Raffa said, throwing her with his change of gear. He stood back, allowing her to go ahead of him. 'I need all the loose ends tied up before I go.'

'Of course.' How stupid was she, thinking Raffa was bringing her upstairs for some sort of romantic tryst? Closing her eyes, she took a moment to reason that at least he was being honest with her. This was all about business. The kiss was just a kiss. Raffa probably handed kisses out like candy. They meant nothing to him. Sexy confidence was simply his default setting. But then he turned, and she hesitated as he held out his hand. It was a moment of decision. There was no mistaking the look in Raffa's eyes. He definitely wanted to sort out the business side of things, but, unless she was very much mistaken, he was offering to sort her out too.

She'd never had a one-night stand. She'd never had any sort of casual relationship. But she would like more of those kisses. And when Raffa smiled into her eyes, as if he were challenging her to go or stay, she was torn between retracing her steps and being bold. The elevator doors were still open. In a couple of steps she could be whisked down to the lobby, where normal service could be resumed: no excitement, no risk, lots of cocoa…

Slipping the lock, he backed Leila through the door of his suite. The bedroom was close, but the sofa was closer. Lowering her onto the cushions, he joined her. She was tiny beneath him, but responsive to the point where she was fierce. He hadn't expected Leila to show quite so much passion, or that she would use her sharp white teeth to nip his skin, and then pluck off her clothes with such abandon. Tugging impatiently at his shirt buttons, she was like a tigress set free from a self-imposed cage. She was innocent, yet deeply sensual, and when he dragged her close and kissed her again her mouth opened under his.

'Do you have any idea how beautiful you are?' he said as she whimpered, wanting more when his stubble raked her skin.

She pulled her head back to look at him. 'Do you have any idea how cheesy that sounds?'

He laughed. 'And you're the quiet sister?'

'Before you came along—'

He didn't let her finish and as his hands mapped the lush curve of her breasts and the smooth line of her thighs she writhed impatiently beneath him. 'Did you wear this underwear with the sole intention of driving me crazy?'

As Raffa was teasing her nipples through the fine fabric of her bra it took her a moment to answer him, and when she gazed down and saw the red filmy lace, she had to admit, 'I'd forgotten that I bought this to…' To build her confidence to face the party, she remembered.

Raffa, dropping kisses on her neck, drew a groaning

response from her throat, and, lacing her fingers through his hair, she kept him close. 'Oh…that's so good.'

'How good?' Raffa demanded, pulling back to look at her.

'Good enough for you not to stop.' Arching her back, she thrust her breasts towards him, wondering what else he could do for other parts of her body. She'd never had such erotic thoughts before and a deep throb of pleasure followed each wicked thought. 'I need you,' she gasped out at one point, hardly knowing what that meant.

'I think I've got that,' Raffa whispered, and when he shifted position she felt how much he wanted her… and when he slipped his fingers beneath the edge of her thong…

'It's almost a shame to take this off.'

'Please don't let that deter you,' she whispered against his mouth.

'That's very forward of you, Leila Skavanga.'

As Raffa was stroking her to a leisurely rhythm, she had no intention of distracting him with any sort of conversation.

'You don't have to do anything,' he promised as he removed what few remaining clothes she had on.

Sounds good to me, she mused, lost in an erotic haze.

'You can safely leave everything to me.'

Safely? And Raffa? Her brain examined this notion sketchily and then drifted away. Leaving everything to him was so good, as was leaving reality behind to pick up another day. Theirs was such a crazy pairing she knew it could never happen again. By the time she visited his island it would be all about business. They'd forget this had ever happened.

Hopefully.

She sighed with pleasure as Raffa feathered kisses

down her neck, to her nipples and on to the area marked danger at the apex of her thighs. She had never been so aware, or so aroused before. And when Raffa teased her lips apart with his tongue…and when he tumbled her beneath him… 'You're impossible,' she exclaimed softly when he did something amazing with his hands.

'So I've been told,' he agreed, sounding not one bit concerned about it.

'I don't want to hear what anyone else said.'

'There is no one else, Leila.'

'For now.'

'There is no one else,' Raffa repeated, staring her straight in the eyes.

'And I'm in control.'

'Absolutely,' Raffa confirmed as she did battle with his belt.

The leather was like butter and she freed the tine in seconds. Whipping the belt from its loops, she was left with a classy horn button and a zipper to tangle with…

'Giving up so easily?' Raffa mocked when she pulled back.

'Just taking a moment.'

In control? Her shaking voice gave her away. She was losing courage with every second that passed. Raffa was so experienced. And she wasn't even a bit experienced where this was concerned.

'Take as long as you want,' he suggested. 'It all adds to the suspense.'

It might take rather longer for the pay-off than he imagined.

'Or would you rather be seduced than be the seducer?'

Thankfully, Raffa didn't wait for her answer. Swinging her into his arms, he carried her into his bedroom, where he laid her down on his enormous bed, his laughing eyes smiling into hers as he kissed her neck…

It was even better when he pinned her wrists above her head. Leave it all to him? She was more than happy to do so.

It wasn't so much a case of seducing Leila, but more of holding her back. His lightest touch sent her over the edge. She was so aroused he had to curb his intentions and go as slowly as he could, which wasn't as easy when Leila Skavanga was the most desirable woman he'd ever known. Her hunger added to her seductive lure and fired his appetite, so that what had begun as an intriguing encounter was transformed into a challenging exercise in restraint for him. His only regret was that there wasn't enough time for them to enjoy each other for as long as he would like.

'Don't stop! Don't you dare stop,' Leila warned him when he drew back. Guiding his hand, she was quite open about what she wanted. He could feel the heat of her need without exploring, and he had to tell her to slow down as he felt around for his jacket.

'I said, don't stop,' she complained, grabbing on to him impatiently.

'And I say we need to take a minute.'

He kissed her into compliance, but he was lost too. He wanted this woman—and not just for easy sex. His hunger defied reason. Wanting Leila had hit him like a freight train. He had never felt this with any woman. And he wanted Leila to want him as he wanted her. He wanted to ride her into Hades and back as he watched pleasure unfold on her face and felt her body bloom beneath him. He wanted to burn his brand into her mind, so there could never be anyone else—

'And I'm bad?' he murmured, when, finally losing patience with him taking so much time to protect them both, Leila grabbed hold of his hand to urge him on.

'You make me bad.'

'Weak argument,' he countered, feeling dangerous heat rush through him as Leila laced her hands around his neck, trusting him with that one small gesture.

'We make each other bad,' she amended, smiling as he drew her into his arms.

Now that he wouldn't argue with. There was something between them he couldn't explain, a fire like nothing he'd ever experienced before. He'd barely touched her before she flew screaming over the edge again, forcing him to hold her firmly in place as, lost to pleasure, she bucked mindlessly beneath him. When she'd calmed down, he smiled. 'This could be a long night, Señorita Skavanga.'

'I certainly hope so,' she said groggily, but then, slowly coming round, she pulled back to look at him and her cheeks flushed red.

'There's no need to apologise for enthusiasm where sex is concerned,' he assured her, kissing her to reassure her as he stroked her hair to soothe her down. 'But if you'd like me to stop—'

'No,' she said fiercely. 'Don't you dare stop.'

Laughing, he dropped kisses on her mouth. This was turning from intriguing to extraordinary. Leila was unique in his experience—unique in the way she made him feel. Why shouldn't they make a habit of this? She should come to his island and stay there.

And he needed a complication like that?

No. But when Leila nestled into the crook of his arm, she was so alluring he had to remind himself forcibly that he'd seen the damage relationships could cause firsthand—the boredom setting in, the unreasonable ties people put on each other, the tragedy of children no one had planned and no one wanted. To see those children shunted back and forth, never really spending time with their parents, but just living their lives with a series of childminders and nannies—

'Raffa?'

'I'm still with you,' he confirmed with a wry smile.

Seeing Leila resting so trustingly in his arms with her eyes full of concern for him prompted him to drop a kiss on the tip of her nose. It was hardly the prelude to a night of wild sex, but, for once in his life, he wasn't sure that was what he wanted, though he had never wanted a woman more.

What was he thinking? Leila had no place in his highly engineered existence, a life that he had polished to his liking over all his adult years. He had created the world's largest chain of fine jewellery stores, with offices across the world, and thousands of people depended on him to get it right. He couldn't afford to squander time on a woman, any woman, even if that woman was Leila Skavanga—especially Leila, who was so young and trusting, and who had her whole life ahead of her. So whatever he imagined he was feeling for her at this moment, he had to remember that his heart was an engine to power his body and nothing more. There was no room in that heart for feelings let alone a self-indulgence like Leila Skavanga. But before he had chance to think about the consequences of involving his emotions, Leila surprised him again and he sucked in a sharp breath as her small hand found him, guided him. Where was his much vaunted self-control now?

'Are you sure?' He felt bound to ask her.

'I've never been more certain of anything in my life,' she said, her gaze steady on his.

He had never been more careful in his life. He wanted Leila to enjoy every moment, and stopped immediately when she whimpered, to ask if she was all right.

'Yes,' she confirmed, moving in a way that drew him deeper.

He wanted to savour the incredible sensation, but Leila was impatient, and, cupping her buttocks, he positioned her. 'Still okay?' he murmured, moving deeper.

'Is it supposed to be this good?'

'I guess,' he whispered against her mouth, 'or why would everyone want to do it?'

'With you?' Her eyes flicked wide open.

'There are other men.'

'Are there?' she gasped, half laughing on a shaking breath as he began to move. She clung to him, her face flushed, her lips parted to drag in air. 'I had no idea it would be this good,' she admitted when he paused to enjoy being so deeply lodged inside her. 'I feel—'

She didn't get chance to tell him how she felt before falling off the edge of the cliff with a wail of surprise, and as she bucked convulsively it took all his ingenuity to keep her beneath him so she could enjoy the experience to the full.

'Incredible!' she exclaimed, panting as she came down. 'You're amazing—'

He laughed as he nuzzled her neck with his stubble. 'And you're a very hungry woman, Leila Skavanga.'

'You noticed?' she said, starting to smile as he dropped kisses on her mouth.

His answer was to move again. As far as he was concerned, it was Leila who was amazing.

'More,' she insisted when they'd been in bed so long dawn was starting to streak the sky with silver.

'I should get up.' He said this reluctantly, conscious of the long flight ahead of him. 'I have to pack before I leave. And I have to file a flight plan before the wedding.'

'Show-off,' she teased him groggily.

He only had to look into Leila's eyes to want to change his mind and postpone his flight. *Dios!* She made him want to postpone the rest of his life to be with her.

'Stay,' she said softly, sensing this hesitation in him. 'Stay with me in Skavanga, Raffa. Why not?'

'I'd love nothing more, but—'

'But you can't,' she said with resignation.

What could he say? He had a life to get back to, as did Leila. 'When you come out to the island—'

Reaching up, she silenced him with her fingertips on his lips. 'Don't say it, Raffa. I know. You have your life and I have mine. This was one very special night—but that's all it is. When I come out to the island I'll be visiting for business and for nothing else. You can rely on me to keep my side of the bargain, as I hope I can rely on you to respect the professional relationship between us. And at the wedding, I'd rather we just kept it light, if that's all right with you. I don't want my sisters getting upset—not today of all days. I must have Britt onside, as technically Britt employs me to run the museum for the Skavanga mining company, so it's important she takes my visit to the island as seriously as I do.'

'I understand.' She'd made it easy for him, which perversely only made him feel worse.

Leila was lying back on the pillows staring blankly ahead, being brave about this as she had been brave about so many other things in her life. How many times had he spent the night with a woman and felt nothing but relief when she left him in the morning? That was most decidedly not how he felt now. 'Go— Go and have your shower,' he prompted. 'Don't make yourself late for your sister's wedding.'

It was over, Leila reflected as she swung out of bed. Their incredible night was over.

'You're still coming to the island?' Raffa confirmed as she reached the door.

'Of course,' she said steadily. 'Nothing's changed.'

But it had and they both knew it.

CHAPTER FIVE

EVERYTHING IN HER life had changed since meeting Raffa. Take this flight to his island. Britt had bumped her up to business class for the first leg of the journey, which had always been one of Leila's ambitions, but the space and pampering only gave her too much time to think about Raffa, and how much she'd missed him.

And how much she had to tell him.

Shifting restlessly in her seat, she took her thoughts back to the wedding. They'd hardly spoken during the day. She'd been busy with bridesmaid's duties, while Raffa had been forced to leave early to make his flight. Some internal warning system had alerted her to the moment he left, and the dreadful sinking sense of loss she had experienced then had never left her. Maybe it never would. Professional relationship? Just the thought of the pledge they'd made to maintain a professional relationship between them seemed like so much nonsense now. Perhaps Raffa could accept it, but then he didn't know—

'It's time to fasten your seat belt, Señorita Skavanga.'

Jolted out of her troubled thoughts by the friendly young flight attendant standing at her side, Leila apologised and quickly fastened her seat belt. 'I didn't see you there. I was...' Daydreaming, Leila silently supplied.

'Welcome to Isla Montaña de Fuego, *señorita*.'

The Island of the Mountains of Fire. How appropriate. Staring out of the small window, she experienced a huge and extremely inconvenient swell of love for Raffa.

And had to mask those feelings. Raffa must know she was completely in control when they met up, and that meant no lingering glances, no longing, no nothing.

To dull the ache inside her, she turned her attention to the view outside the window as the plane came in to land. Seen from this height, Raffa's island retreat was surprisingly lush and green. A deep ivory band of sand bordered a bright blue sea on one side of the island, while on the other coastline an angry sea lashed a range of dramatic black rocks. The contrast was glaring. The young cabin attendant explained that they would be landing in the north of the island. 'The south is softer, and has fabulous golden beaches,' she went on, dipping her head to follow Leila's gaze out of the window.

Leila instantly pictured Raffa's fortress home being in the north, where it would be well barricaded from the world between forbidding mountains and a ferocious sea. 'Why don't you sit with me for landing, Elena?' There was so much more she wanted to know about the island and about the man who lived here…the man with whom, quite incredibly, she was expecting a baby.

'Where exactly is the castle?' she asked as soon as Elena was safely buckled in.

'Don Leon's home is in the south of the island.'

When Leila expressed surprise, Elena explained. 'The reasoning in the old days was that because of the treacherous rocks in the north, that part of the island was impregnable and could take care of itself, while the south was soft and vulnerable. So that's where Don Leon's ancestors built their castle.'

It made perfect sense, which was more than could be said for Leila's current state of mind.

'The castle is absolutely stunning,' Elena went on. 'Don Leon has been working so hard on it for years. Have you seen it yet?'

'No, I haven't.' Leila looked at Elena with renewed interest. The young girl was very pretty.

And why was she behaving like a jealous lover? It was time to put this pointless longing for Raffa Leon out of her head for good.

But how could she ever cut him out of her life now?

Elena interrupted Leila's thoughts with some more information about the castle. 'It's not forbidding at all. Don Leon has done so much of the work himself and he invites his staff each year for a party so we can see how the work is progressing. He's such a generous man.'

So much for the press dubbing him ruthless. Turmoil at the thought that this was the man Leila had always dreamed of fathering the child she had always longed for, combined with the guilt she felt at not having been able to locate Raffa before she arrived to let him know she had just discovered she was pregnant, was making her edgy and frustrated.

'I believe Don Leon's design studios are over here on the island?' she babbled, as if she didn't know they were, in a hopeless attempt to take her mind off the man and the consequences of their one night of passion.

'We'll fly over them soon. Is that where you'll be working?' Elena asked pleasantly.

Thankfully, Elena couldn't know about the turmoil in Leila's mind. 'Most probably.'

She couldn't even be sure of that. She had sent repeated mails to Raffa's headquarters in an attempt to contact him, and had finally introduced herself to his team via HR, but when she explained her ideas for an exhibition in Skavanga, she was told Don Leon would decide her agenda. But where was he? No one would tell her, and her tireless investigations had drawn a blank.

'And there he is,' Elena exclaimed, shocking Leila back into the present.

As the jet touched down and screamed along the runway Leila had the briefest glimpse of an unmistakeable figure. Lounging back against a Jeep, Raffa Leon, exactly as she remembered him: powerful, hard, self-avowed bachelor by preference, a man who had no intention of having children to disturb his smooth-running life.

If only he'd sent a driver so she could have had some time to compose herself. She longed to see him again, but dreaded this first meeting. She dreaded what she might see in Raffa's eyes. Nothing would be terrible. Intuition would be worse. She had to tell him her news before he could find out for himself.

And what would Raffa see in her eyes? Guilt? He would want to know why she hadn't told him the moment she knew she was pregnant. Why she hadn't emblazoned it in the sky. 'I had to speak to you in person' would sound lame in the face of the shock he was going to get.

Pausing at the top of the aircraft steps, she braced herself for their first encounter. 'How often are these flights?' she asked the young flight attendant as Raffa closed the distance between them in a few long strides.

'We fly whenever Don Leon sends for the plane,' Elena explained. 'There is no other way off the island. No ferries could possibly dock in the north. As you've seen, the coastline is too rugged. And the south is all helicopters and private yachts—most of which belong to Don Leon, or to his company.'

So she was stuck on Raffa's island, with no way off, other than with his permission. Why hadn't she thought ahead about this, and arranged to meet him on neutral ground?

'Leila…'

Too late now.

The familiar voice washed over her, the rich, deep tones disarming her and making her forget everything except seeing Raffa again, though she registered now that his manner was carefully judged and disappointingly neutral.

'Raffa…'

Coming down the steps, she extended her hand to greet him, matching his businesslike manner with a cool air of her own. 'It's good to see you again.'

'And you, Leila.'

He ignored her hand and removed his sunglasses.

That penetrating stare… Those incredible eyes could search her soul. Could he see the truth?

She looked away, but not before she noticed the speculation in his stare. Raffa missed nothing. He could read the smallest shift in body language and never took anything for granted. He was scanning her now for any sign of emotion to suggest she was a clinging vine who might make demands on him after what had happened between them at the party.

Composing herself, she lifted her chin to meet his gaze. Britt had mentioned the fact that Raffa's questing nature had contributed massively to his success, and that he was unparalleled when it came to spotting things other people missed, and that this was what kept him so far ahead of the pack. She would do well to remember that.

'You're well, Leila?'

Her cheeks flushed red at that simple question. Well? She was blooming. 'Yes, very well, thank you. You?'

He nodded briefly.

Raffa looked amazing, in nothing more than a pair of worn jeans and a dark, close-fitting top. She inhaled a faint tang of his cologne. He was standing so close she could see the amber flecks in his sepia eyes and feel his familiar power warming her. It was impossible to forget what had happened between them, or the consequences of their one night together.

'Let me carry your case,' he said, reaching for her bag.

'I can manage, thank you.'

'You don't have to manage, Leila.'

Raffa sounded faintly impatient and she couldn't blame him as she thought back to the last time they'd seen each other—glimpsed each other, really, across a crowded ballroom at Eva's wedding. She'd been too busy to speak to him, and yet the night before she'd been lost in his arms—wild in his arms. And now the consequences of that night, consequences that Raffa didn't know about yet, would have to be brought out into the open and discussed. There was an awkward time ahead of them, to say the least.

She followed him to the Jeep, determined she would keep her head, but once the doors closed and they were contained in the small cab she was all too aware of the tension swirling round them.

'You're very quiet,' Raffa remarked as he started the engine. 'Don't you have any news for me, Leila?'

'About the museum?' Her throat tightened on the question.

'Of course about the museum.' Slipping his sunglasses on, Raffa put the vehicle into gear and released the brake.

Of course. What else could they possibly have to talk about? The conversation between them was so stilted and awkward, she wasn't sure she could rescue the situation. Bracing her arm against the dashboard as Raffa bumped the Jeep over the rutted track that led to the highway, she glanced at his rugged face in profile. There was no softness in his expression. 'Did you see the mail I sent you?'

'Mail?' He frowned, his swarthy features more forbidding than ever. 'What mail?'

'The mail I sent to your company in advance of my arrival here. The mail I sent to introduce myself to your team. I copied you in.'

Raffa's frown deepened.

No one got under her skin as he did, and far from being the peacemaker, her usual role back home, she was screaming inside and had to say something. 'Were you ever going to read it?'

Pulling his head back, Raffa flashed a glance across at her. 'If it's in my inbox I'll get round to it.'

'Raffa, you disappeared off the face of the earth. Where've you been?'

'Tied up, looking after my grandmother. She hasn't been well recently.'

She went hot with embarrassment for misjudging him so badly. 'I'm so sorry. I hope she's feeling better now.'

Guilt flashed through her as Raffa responded with a curt nod of his head. With her own concerns banging in her brain, she hadn't paused to think why he might be off radar.

There had been a stack of mail waiting for him, but with his mind on Abuelita he hadn't even glanced at it.

His grandmother was supposed to be indestructible. She wasn't supposed to get sick. That wasn't Leila's fault, but there was something about Leila making him edgy. She'd changed. He couldn't put his finger on it yet, but he would. He reasoned that seeing her again had thrown him badly. He had thought he could handle it, but now he wasn't so sure.

'In future, I'll make certain your mail hits the top of the stack,' he offered for the sake of building a working relationship.

'Thank you, Raffa.'

Even that bland response made him suspicious. Leila was too mild—so mild she made him curious as to why. The Leila he knew was quiet, but she stood up for herself, and was feisty and fun. This Leila was guarded and distant. Keeping up a business front couldn't account for such a complete change in anyone.

Keeping up a business front wouldn't be easy for either of them, he conceded. It was hard for him to find a comfortable operating zone with a woman who had been his lover and who was now a colleague. It would have been easier with anyone other than Leila, because most women didn't want what she wanted from him; they were far more calculating. But Leila had always been quite open about wanting the whole nine yards: the happy ending, the home, the children—not quite sure about the doting husband, though she deserved nothing less. But none of that was in his gift. He was a confirmed bachelor who had learned to curb his feelings from a young age.

'Seeing as you haven't received my mail, I hope you won't think my ideas for the exhibition too ambitious, Raffa.'

Again he detected tension in her voice and wondered at it. 'Nothing you ever did could surprise me, Leila.'

She looked away, when he had only been trying to lighten the atmosphere. Now he was certain she was hiding something. 'Twenty minutes and we'll be there,' he said, wondering which of them longed to reach their destination more.

She was here to work, Leila reminded herself firmly. Raffa didn't have to be the man she remembered. She didn't expect him to be. And she would have plenty of chances while she was on the island to tell him she was pregnant. If they were going to work together she had to put things back on track before she tackled anything personal.

'I'm looking forward to learning more about your gems.'

Dipping his head briefly to register the fact that he'd heard her was Raffa's only response.

She couldn't leave it at that. She had to straighten things out between them. 'I realise you're far more sophisticated than I am, but—'

'Let me put you out of your misery, Leila.' He said this coolly, not even glancing at her as he concentrated on the road ahead. 'You're here to work and so am I. I'm not on your agenda and you're not on mine. Not in the personal sense, anyway. Does that reassure you?'

Her stomach clenched at Raffa's words. He couldn't have made it any plainer that he didn't want any reminders of their brief and passionate encounter. 'I am reassured,' she lied, her mind full of the baby. How could she tell him now?

She had to find a way to tell him. It was as simple as that.

They drove in tense silence for quite a time. She

stared blindly out of the window, but the incredible view finally pierced her sombre mood. Raffa's island home was beautiful and she couldn't remain immune to it. The jet hadn't flown over this part of the island. The agricultural land was lush and well cared for, and on the fringes of the rolling fields immaculately maintained farmsteads slumbered in the sun. He drove on through quaint villages, where white villas nestled in companionable groups on tree-cloaked hills, until finally he turned to her and said, 'This is the village where I live.'

She looked with interest at the cobbled streets and a tiny market square, where stalls selling fresh produce from outlying farms were bustling with activity. As they passed through the village they drove on along a clifftop road where she could see the bright blue sea glinting far below them. 'This is lovely,' she exclaimed impulsively, relaxing for the first time since she'd arrived.

'Wait until you see the castle. There—on the top of the hill.'

Seeing their destination loom in front of her made all of Leila's fears return. If only Raffa already knew about the baby, and they could celebrate her pregnancy together—not that he was ever likely to celebrate, with his thoughts on the subject.

She turned to look at him as he launched into a brief history of the ancient building he was working so hard to save, and found herself wishing she didn't have any secrets from him so she could relax and enjoy this trip to the full.

Her biggest surprise was when they drove beneath the imposing stone archway that led through from the outer walls of the castle into the inner courtyard. Instead of closing around her as she had expected, being inside the ancient fortress actually lifted her spirits. The castle might have been built with the sole intention of defending the island from invaders, but it felt more like a friendly giant than a glowering monster.

'Everyone says the same thing,' Raffa agreed when she commented. 'I think it's the angle of the sun on the stone that makes it glow and seem so welcoming.'

At least they were talking, Leila registered with relief. If she could keep that going, maybe the tension between them would relax. Build enough of a bridge and she could have a proper discussion about the baby.

'The same building beneath the steely skies of Skavanga might struggle to look as attractive as this,' she admitted, turning to him.

'You're probably right,' Raffa agreed. 'I hope you're not too disappointed when we go inside, as I only live in a small part of the castle. I'm gradually turning the rest into a museum.'

'Museums are becoming a bit of a theme between us,' she remarked as he switched off the engine. She stopped there, seeing something in Raffa's eyes that warned her off. It said there were no common themes between them.

'I've housed you in one of the guest turrets,' he said as they got out of the Jeep. Shading his eyes with his hand, he stared up to where the crenelated battlements were decorated with flags.

'Like Rapunzel,' she suggested lightly.

'Like someone I thought might enjoy the view.'

'I'm here to work, not to stare out of the window all day,' she reminded him, working hard to keep the conversation between them going. And you're not scrambling up my hair any time soon, she thought as Raffa glanced at her.

'I'll get my housekeeper to help you settle in.' He pulled away as if he was impatient to go.

His housekeeper? The castle, Raffa's whole way of life, only served to emphasise the gulf between them, and she had yet to broach the subject of his child.

'Leila?'

Having climbed the broad flight of stone steps, they had stopped in front of a huge arched entrance door peppered with iron studs. 'Yes?'

She turned, but whatever had prompted Raffa to say her name had died on his lips. She was glad when the door swung open and a smiling motherly woman greeted them.

'This is Maria, my housekeeper, Leila. Maria, may I present Señorita Skavanga.'

'Please, call me Leila,' Leila insisted as the older woman nodded and smiled.

Raffa excused himself almost immediately. 'I have building work to attend to,' he explained.

'Thank you for picking me up—' She turned around to say this, but he was already jogging down the steps.

'May I show you to your room, *señorita?*'

'Thank you, Maria.' She was glad of the housekeeper's friendly smile. She had never felt quite so isolated, or quite so far from home.

Leila's apartment in the turret was like the setting for a fairy tale. Exquisitely furnished in delicate French Empire style, it boasted the most astonishing views over the beautifully manicured grounds to the lush green fields beyond, and on to where a bank of trees faded to a misty purple in the shadow of the rolling hills. Leaning out of the open window, she dragged greedily on the blossom-scented air, but this was no time to be daydreaming. She had to settle in and then find Raffa so they could have that talk. She had never even been late before, and she hadn't even been sure that the strange feeling that had come over her was significant in any way, until finally she went to the chemist and took a test…several tests. And there was no doubt. She was pregnant.

The phone rang, distracting her. It was Raffa. Her heart bumped at the sound of his voice. The knowledge inside her made her feel so guilty, but she couldn't tell him over the phone.

'Can you be ready in half an hour?'

'I'm ready now.' Did that sound too eager?

Of course it did.

Remembering the marble-lined bathroom stocked with fabulous products, she quickly built in time to take a shower. 'Actually, half an hour should be fine,' she managed coolly.

It was only when she replaced the receiver that she realised she hadn't even asked where they were supposed to meet. She would have to sharpen up her wits if she was going to face Raffa with her news. She couldn't imagine he would take it well, and she had to be ready for the fallout.

The rest of the day went better than she had expected. Raffa picked her up in the Jeep and took her to one of his showrooms on the island, but he brought a co-worker with him, so once again she couldn't tell him her news. Would the moment ever arrive? She was keyed up every second of the tour and could hardly concentrate.

The laboratories were as clean and as sterile as Raffa's behaviour towards her. They were bright and filled with light and staffed by uniformed technicians. It was that small space thing again, Leila told herself firmly, glancing at Raffa as they travelled down to one of his vaults in a small steel lift. *Relax*. He can't hear your heart beating.

Raffa escorted her into an air-conditioned room with little furnishing other than a table on which sat a mirror, presumably so his most favoured clients could try on the jewels they wished to buy in absolute privacy. She felt confident, having prepared well in advance of her visit. 'I know many of your jewels have history, and I've read up about quite a few of them.'

Raffa inclined his head as if they were two strangers doing business together, which indeed they were—or they were supposed to be.

He laid out an incredible collection in front of her. 'This can be worn a number of ways,' he explained as he took apart one of the elaborate necklaces. 'These detachable drops can be worn as earrings, for example…'

As he held them up to her face, his hands brushed her cheeks and her skin blazed with awareness. 'Very nice,' she said, turning away so she couldn't see Raffa's face reflected in the mirror behind her.

'And these…' he showed her a string of milky pearls '…can be worn as a long necklace, or fastened with this diamond clasp and worn as a collar…'

He had to hear her sharp intake of breath when his hands brushed her collarbone and the cool pearls met her overheated skin, but when he glanced into her eyes he gave nothing away. The cool of the pearls, the warmth of his touch…

'Leila?'

She blinked and refocused on the tutorial she was supposed to be here for.

'I'm going to put the pearls back in the vault again. If you've finished with them?'

'Yes.' Her throat was dry, her voice hoarse. She could

see Raffa standing behind her, staring down. This was the moment—

'Shall I list the pearls as going to Skavanga?'

Raffa was already turning away as he asked the question, placing the priceless jewels in their velvet nest. The walls of the vault seemed to close around her, sucking all the available air from her lungs and her intention to tell him about the baby with it.

'Yes. Please put them on the list,' she managed faintly.

His preference would have been to strip Leila naked, drape her in jewels and have her on the table, but that was the wolf in him talking, and Leila was a lamb, vulnerable and far too honest for her own good. He had seen the longing in her eyes the moment she arrived on the island. He had finally deciphered what had made him edgy around Leila back at the airstrip, and it was that. And now he knew he couldn't lead her on. They'd had one passionate night and that had been a mistake, a mistake he had no intention of repeating. Leila deserved someone better than he could ever be, someone without his baggage. She had tempted him, but that was over now and she was here to do a job. He would respect that. His father had used women as if they were nothing more than disposable toys, and he had no intention of becoming that man.

'We've done enough for today,' he said, his mind still lodged in the past.

He'd done enough for today. He'd spent enough time with Leila, and he needed space from her now. Seeing her again had been a warning to him that, far from fading, his feelings for Leila Skavanga had only grown while they'd been apart.

CHAPTER SIX

THE NEXT FEW days passed quickly and things evened out between them. Their history was too complex for them to remain at daggers drawn for ever. Close proximity led to them swapping confidences and swapping jokes, but whether it was the intimate, confiding tone Raffa used to explain the provenance of one of the jewels, or whether it was simply his passion for his chosen subject and his vast store of knowledge, Leila had no idea.

Perhaps it was the way he looked into her eyes in search of the same enthusiasm he felt for the treasures he was showing her, she really couldn't say. She only knew she was losing her heart to him all over again, though they went to bed separately each night, and she slept fitfully, wondering if Raffa did too.

As each day dawned she felt more and more convinced that if she could just hold on a little longer, the golden moment would arrive when she could tell Raffa about the baby and they'd both be happy about the news. Being pregnant was such a life-changing event she wanted to be sure she picked the right moment for him too. As she was dealing with a man for whom family life was anything but an attractive prospect, she wanted to make sure she didn't blunder into the announcement.

She hadn't been expecting for them to work so closely

in the physical sense. There were times when tension seemed to surge between them, and she wondered if they were both fighting off desire, and other times when she told herself not to be so stupid. Sometimes she found herself studying Raffa instead of the jewels... Diamonds or his sexy mouth? A polished emerald, or the gleam in the depth of Raffa's eyes when he turned to confide some new fact, especially when he allowed his gaze to linger?

'What are you staring at?' he said one day, smiling.

She'd always been a sucker for eyes that crinkled at the corners. 'You,' she admitted bluntly. 'I was just thinking how different you are from the press you receive.'

'We all have different faces we show the world,' he said as he collected up the jewels for the night.

'And you have more than most?' she queried, laughing to make light of it.

'Here's one that might surprise you,' he said as he closed the vault. 'I'm immune to the charm of diamonds. I admire them. I admire the craftsmanship. And I know a good stone when I see one. But I prefer the simple things in life—like honesty and loyalty. I value those qualities far more than any hard, cold stone. Diamonds are just a means to an end for me. I make money out of them that allows me to support the causes I'm interested in.'

Honesty and loyalty, she thought as Raffa called the elevator. Where would Raffa think she stood where honesty was concerned if he knew about the baby?

'The exhibition you're planning in Skavanga will be good for both of us,' he said as they waited for the lift to arrive. 'I almost threw my first diamond away— After you.' He stood back as the doors slid open. He stabbed the lift button and they soared upwards. 'My father, who wasn't noted for his tolerance, brought a particularly big stone back from India. I didn't know the value of this dull-looking rock and kept it in my bedroom for over a week before he found it.'

She laughed, but it sounded forced. She would rather have been talking about the subject closest to her heart, until Raffa said, 'My father was always mad with one child or another.' His eyes narrowed as he thought back, remembering. 'We children hadn't been factored into his life plan. We were more of an inconvenience to him than anything else. An inconvenient consequence of his own reckless actions—'

Her heart shrank as she listened to him. They'd both been reckless, but if she had anything to do with it their baby would be anything but an inconvenient consequence. It would be a much-loved child.

'My family isn't close like yours is, Leila,' he went on. 'I don't have a great role model to look back on, hence no wife, no children and no intention on my part of ever changing the status quo.'

'So you don't want children?' Her question echoed in the small steel cab.

'No. I don't,' Raffa said flatly. 'I've told you things I haven't told anyone before,' Raffa admitted wryly as they walked outside into the brilliant sunshine. 'Must be your honest face.'

'I'll respect your confidence.' Her stomach churned at the thought of her less than honest relationship with Raffa.

'I'm sure you will. And I apologise if I sounded short down there. I didn't mean to.'

'The past kicks back sometimes. Raffa, there's—'

He broke off to speak to one of the technicians walking across the car park. They were all coming out for lunch now, and when he turned back to her the moment had gone.

'I trust you, Leila Skavanga. I can't say that about many people.'

This was getting worse by the moment. 'I trust you too,' she said on a dry throat, only wishing she could turn the clock back and blurt out the truth about their baby the moment she walked down the steps of the aircraft.

'Let's get back,' he said. 'I'm hungry, aren't you?'

'Starving.'

'Then I have to get back to my building work. I hope you've learned enough this morning to keep you busy planning.'

'Absolutely,' she confirmed. Raffa telling her about his past had explained so much about him. He was obsessive about his work at the castle, the ruin he was rebuilding brick by brick, perhaps as an exercise in pushing the memories of his crumbling childhood behind him. This was not the time to raise the subject of a child, however much it would be loved, that was going to be born as the result of yet another reckless coupling.

'We've got a fair moving into the grounds of the castle tomorrow,' he revealed as they approached the Jeep. 'I'll be up early sorting that out—so have breakfast without me.'

'Don't worry about me,' she said as he opened the door for her. 'I can entertain myself. Is the fair part of your plan to open more of the castle to the public?'

'That's right,' Raffa said as he swung into the driver's seat beside her.

This was better than being at daggers drawn with him. She would find a way to tell Raffa about the baby, but it would be a way that wouldn't pour more acid on the wounds he'd brought with him from his past. Perhaps friendship was the only way forward for them, she thought wistfully, flashing a glance across, but, as she'd always been wary of expecting too much out of life, wasn't it better to settle for less and be contented?

She woke the next morning feeling warm inside. The baby made her feel this way. Nothing could dilute her joy, not even the guilt inside her. She could already picture the infant with Raffa's curly black hair and his slanting smile. If it was a boy he would eat her out of house and home, and scare her rigid with his pranks. If it was a little girl…

It was to be hoped she had more sense than her mother.

Planning to have a family without factoring a man into the equation was all very well in theory, but she couldn't see Raffa being the type to quietly stand by when she told him about the baby and then let her get on with it. She would tell him today. She couldn't leave it a moment longer. Her heart had grown to encompass a new and very special kind of love and she wanted Raffa to know that joy too. There hadn't been a good time to tell him, so she would make an opportunity. She was confident he would be thrilled—once he got over the shock.

Frantically finger-combing her hair into some sort of order, she hurried out of the room, having decided that the best place to find Raffa was in the courtyard where he had said the fair was setting up.

The courtyard was bustling with shoppers from all over the island, and noisy with stallholders calling out to advertise their wares. She walked around it several times, but there was no sign of Raffa, and so she started to take a more active interest in the stalls. One geared specifically towards baby clothes drew her attention right away. The tiny, hand-stitched garments were so adorable that before she knew it her arms were full.

'Leila?'

She paled as Raffa took in everything at a glance. 'I didn't see you there.'

'Clearly.'

Her heart sank. Of all the opportunities she'd had, this was the worst possible moment. Her guilty face gave everything away and she could feel anger coming off him in waves. 'Raffa, I—'

'Let me get those,' he interrupted. Turning his back on her, he spoke to the woman manning the stall, reverting to Spanish as he completed the transaction, effectively cutting Leila out so all she could do was stand back, feeling useless.

Feeling worse than useless. Everyone on the island loved Raffa. They trusted him. He had said he trusted her. How did he feel about that now? What would these people—Raffa's people—think of her? She only had to watch the way they responded to Raffa to know they loved him. He'd done so much for them, creating employment and bringing the island to life again. And she was a nobody carrying his child, a child she didn't even have the guts to tell him about.

'Thank you,' she said automatically when Raffa swung around with her purchases. 'I'll give you the money.' She held out her hand with a bundle of notes, but Raffa ignored them and directed a hard, knowing stare into her eyes instead.

'Have you had some happy news from one of your sisters?' he suggested in an icy tone. 'Or a friend, perhaps?'

Her shocked look answered everything he wanted to know.

'You're ominously silent, Leila. Are you buying baby clothes with an eye on the future?'

Her throat was in knots. It should be so easy to tell him her news, but she'd left it too long to do so.

'Well?' Raffa prompted coldly. 'Don't you have anything to say to me?'

This was so far removed from how she had imagined it would be when she told Raffa about the child they were expecting. She had intended to tell him quietly, confidently, with the aim of reassuring Raffa that she expected nothing from him.

'Well, it's a very nice gift, anyway,' he said, hoisting up the bags up so they met her eyeline. 'A very generous gift, in fact—so many outfits.'

'I need to talk to you, Raffa. Can we go inside?'

A brief dip of his head was Raffa's only response.

Was this the friend she'd thought she'd made, the tender lover who had helped create the child inside her? She had taken far too much for granted. She hadn't known Raffa was overshadowed by his past, or what had gone into the construction of his new life. No children, he'd said. No children he'd meant. But as she planned to bring up their child alone, she was sure she could make things right between them—if only he would give her the chance to explain.

Cold anger filled him. He had trusted Leila. He had confided in Leila as he had never confided in anyone before. And now this greatest truth of all and she had shut him out. How long had she known about the baby? When they'd been laughing and growing closer as they worked together, had she known then? Had she known before she came to the island? He always took precautions, and had assumed—

Assume nothing. This was not the time to curse his uncharacteristic lack of caution. He had to know the truth. The thought that Leila might be scheming to trap him into some sort of arrangement tore him apart. Surely, she couldn't have planned this, but could he trust his own judgement when wanting Leila was a madness he couldn't control? He'd seduced her shamelessly, only to discover she had more passion in her than any woman he'd ever known. He'd lit that fire. And now he must live with the consequences.

A baby. His child. Incredible. Why hadn't she told him before now?

He could hardly wait until he'd shut the world out of his study before rounding on her. 'You must have known you were pregnant before you came here.'

'You make it sound as if I planned this.'

'Well, didn't you?' Crossing his arms over his chest, he leaned back against the desk to view her from his great height, but instead of shrinking from him Leila grew in stature and took him on.

'There's no plan here. I was waiting for the right time to tell you.'

'The right time,' he echoed. 'Tell me, Leila—when is the right time?'

'Don't,' she warned him. 'I'm not asking for anything from you. I'm quite capable of bringing up a child by myself.'

'I don't doubt it. Wasn't that your intention all along? Didn't you tell me when we met at Britt's party that you wanted children, but you didn't want the man?'

'That was just talk and you know it.'

'Was it, Leila? How do I know it was just talk when

I don't know you? I thought I was coming to know you, but I was wrong. Most women are open about what they want from me—'

'And I'm not?' she cut in.

'They ask—they get—they tell me what they're prepared to give me in return.'

A shudder ran through her. 'I feel sorry for you, Raffa, taking part in such cold-blooded transactions.'

'Grow up, Leila! We had sex. It was one night. It was never meant to be a lifetime commitment—'

'But there was always that possibility—'

'A possibility you hoped for.'

'No!'

'A possibility that could certainly have been avoided if you'd kept your legs closed—'

'And you'd kept your pants on,' she fired back. Launching herself at him, she tried to wrestle the bags from his hand. 'Give them to me and I'll happily go—'

'Go where?' he derided, holding them out of her reach. 'Are you going to swim home?'

'I'll find some way to leave your island,' she assured him, face tense, jaw clenched, her lips white with rage.

'We've got a few things to sort out first, Leila—'

'There's nothing for you to sort out. I wanted to tell you. I wanted to explain gently—'

He laughed in her face. 'What? So you could help me to get over the shock? I don't even know if it's my child!'

'Of course it's your child! I was a virgin—'

'What?'

Raffa's reaction stunned her. Hand over his face as if he couldn't bear to look at her, he was clearly appalled.

'What did you say?' Lowering his hand, he stared at her in disbelief.

'I was a virgin when I met you, and there's never been anyone else.'

She'd never known Raffa lost for words, but the way he looked now, bemused and drained of all emotion, was more frightening to see than any anger or derision of his could ever be.

'You lost your virginity with me,' he said, staring at her intently as if he had to get this fact set absolutely firm in his mind.

'Yes.' Her voice wavered. Her eyes filled with tears. The air around them was like a void, a black hole in space. And there was no way across that void, no way at all.

This was his worst nightmare come true. He had stolen the most precious gift Leila had to give without even knowing it. And now a child would be born as a consequence of his actions. Parents at war on opposites sides of an unbridgeable divide was his worst nightmare.

Consequences were a daily concern for him in business. He never made a move without planning forward first, but he had never had to factor such an almighty screw-up into his thinking before.

'Don't look at me like that,' Leila begged him. 'This isn't what you think, Raffa.'

'What do I think?'

'I don't know.' Leila searched for the right words to say. 'Maybe you think I planned this? With your wealth and title I can understand—'

'I thought that would raise its head at some point,' he said angrily, though deep down he knew Leila cared nothing for his wealth and title, but he was too shaken up to stop. Nothing rocked him, nothing touched him, but this had. She had.

Pressing her lips together in despair, she shook her

head. 'That's just it, Raffa. Your status doesn't mean anything to me. I care about you, Raffa. I care about you—Raffa—the man. I even fooled myself into thinking we were growing close, could become friends—'

'How convenient!' He wanted to slam his hands over his ears so he didn't have to listen to any more of this. 'What form would this friendship take, Leila? Was it designed to butter me up before you told me you were expecting my child?'

'I haven't engineered any of this, Raffa—'

'So you say.' Leila's voice had deepened with emotion and the expression on her face shamed him, but his circuit board was overloaded and what he needed most of all now was time and space away from her to think.

'I can't make you believe me, Raffa. I know the truth, and that will have to be enough for me. I must focus on my child. And right now?' Heaving a sigh, she shook her head. 'I'm not sure I want you to be part of my child's life.'

'That's not your choice to make, Leila.'

'Don't look at me like that,' she begged him quietly. 'I won't stand here and take your contempt, Raffa. I might not be anything special, but I'm not a piece of dirt attached to your shoe either.'

'How should I behave towards you, Leila?' His head was still ringing with everything she'd told him. 'Like the love of my life? Like a woman I've known for years and have planned to have a baby with? Or a woman I slept with once, who gets herself knocked up?'

The slap came out of nowhere.

Seizing her wrist an instant before her hand connected with his face, he held her motionless in front of him as a bolt of fury flashed between them.

'I don't expect either of those things,' she assured

him in a low, cold voice. 'I expect you to treat me with the respect due to the mother of your child, and nothing more. I don't expect anything from you in the material sense. I never have, and I never will.'

'Really?' He almost laughed.

'Don't mock me, Raffa. And don't judge me by the standards of anyone else you might have known. Whatever you think of me, I won't allow you to ride roughshod over me.'

'So what do you want, Leila?'

'Nothing. Not from you,' she assured him with icy calm. 'I'm going to keep this baby and be a single mother like so many other women, and I'll get by.'

'Without me in the picture?' He laughed. 'You *are* naïve.'

'Naïve, Raffa? Or does the fact that I don't need you hurt your pride?'

He ground his jaw as a very real and primal fear rose up inside him. Reason had no part to play in that fear and it was centred around the birth of his child, and the safety of the woman in front of him. 'I don't remember you consulting me about any of this,' he said as blood pounded in his head.

'I don't need to consult you, Raffa. I'm not your employee. This is my body and my baby.'

'Our baby,' he shot back. 'There's a very good reason for my not wanting children—'

'Well, why don't you tell me what it is?' she exclaimed.

No. He could never do that. The guilt haunted him. It disabled him. 'All you need to know is that I don't want children. I never have and I never will, and this little surprise of yours hasn't changed anything.'

'Can't you explain why you feel so strongly?' Leila begged him.

As she reached out to touch him he pulled away. 'You have no idea what you've done.'

Shaking her head slowly, Leila raised her wounded gaze to his face. 'So what are you suggesting, Raffa?' she asked him quietly. 'Are you asking me to get rid of this baby?'

He reeled mentally at Leila's mistaken interpretation of his words. 'What type of man do you take me for?'

'That's just it, Raffa. I don't know what kind of man you are. I thought I did, but I was wrong. I don't understand why you're so set against having children. Is it me?'

'No, it's…'

'I can't understand why you're so horrified at the idea of me giving birth,' Leila exclaimed with frustration when he fell silent. 'And if you won't tell me—'

'I won't tell you, because it's none of your damn business. I've told you more than enough already.'

'Because we trust each other,' she insisted, staring up into his rigid face. 'Or we did.'

'Trust takes time to build, Leila, and can be lost in a heartbeat.'

'Is that what happened to us, Raffa?'

'What do you think?'

Raffa's words were like a series of slaps hitting her in the face. By the time they both fell silent her head was reeling with confusion and hurt. This was the last thing she had wanted when she told Raffa about the baby. They had shared so many things, and they had grown close while she'd been on the island; that wasn't an illusion. Friendship might have taken over from passion, she was quite prepared to admit that, but both were dead now.

And she had so wanted this to be a special and tender moment between them. If only she could get to the bottom of Raffa's horror at the thought of her giving birth. If only she could bring him back to her. His behaviour was so unreasonable there had to be something more eating away at him, but unless he was prepared to tell her, they would never be close again.

Her hand moved instinctively to cover her stomach, as if she could protect the tiny life from all the emotion swirling round it. 'The last thing I had intended was to upset you, or shock you. I kept waiting for the right moment—the perfect moment, but it must have passed me by. Please forgive me.'

He didn't reply. He couldn't reply. He was empty inside. He closed off from feeling because he didn't know any other way. He had lived behind emotional barricades since he was a child. How could he ever be a fit parent? His life didn't allow for children. He was always driving forward to seize the next opportunity, or to close the next deal.

'Parents at war are my worst nightmare,' Leila said, echoing his own thoughts on the subject. 'But perhaps we can be friends, Raffa. And if you really don't want any part in this, wouldn't it be better for me to return to Skavanga without any more fuss?'

'Fuss?' Repeating the word, he tossed it around in his mind. He wanted all the fuss in the world to surround Leila on the day she gave birth. 'And you want to go back to Skavanga?' he said distractedly, already making plans to appoint the top people in their field to attend her—but here. Here on the island.

'In your current mood,' she said quietly, 'I'd be relieved.'

He was slowly coming out of the dark tunnel into the

light, from the past to the present, and now he was fully focused on Leila he couldn't believe how controlled she was, how calm. But Leila had always been the one fixed point in a turbulent sea of siblings.

And the child had changed her. It had given her a new inner strength. No more the mouse in the shadow of her siblings, Leila had emerged as a warrior in defence of her child. But if she thought she could keep this baby away from him and disappear out of his life for good, she was wrong, though he would never promise her more than he was capable of giving. 'I accept full responsibility, of course, but that doesn't change anything between us.'

'I don't expect it to, Raffa.' Leila's gaze remained unswerving on his face. 'I'm quite capable of handling this on my own. I have a duty to tell you, and that is all.'

'How sensible of you.'

'And how cold of you,' she countered, staring at him with concern in her eyes. 'We're talking about a child, Raffa, and yet your manner is so distant we might be discussing a deal you may or may not want to buy into. I'm not sorry this happened. However inconvenient a baby might be for you, I can't wait to hold my first child in my arms. And I will *never* regret being pregnant.'

He held up his hand. 'I promise you that you have nothing to worry about. As far as all the practicalities are concerned I'll have my lawyers draw up a contract between us.'

'A contract?' Leila shook her head. 'That's your answer to everything, isn't it, Raffa? Get the lawyers to deal with it—delegate, distance yourself, don't engage your emotions in any way. The stroke of a pen is far easier and much safer than risking your heart.'

'You don't know what you're talking about. I pay lawyers to handle my problems.'

'But this isn't a problem,' Leila insisted with a sad laugh in her voice. Embracing her stomach, she added softly, 'This is a baby, Raffa.'

'I delegate so I can get on with the job of keeping thousands of people employed,' he informed her with biting calm. And now he needed space and time to plan. Walking around her, he headed for the door.

'That's right, Raffa—run away!'

He returned in a stride and stood staring down at her, but instead of recoiling she reached out to him. 'I wish I could help you, Raffa.'

'Help me?' He speared a glance at her hands and she lowered them to her sides.

'Perhaps you expected me to be more sophisticated,' she said, stopping him at the door. 'Perhaps you expect me to treat this lightly, to smile prettily and move on, accept a large cheque each month in lieu of your attention, as if I've scored a double—a baby and a wealthy patron.'

'I expect you to be honest with me. Is that too much to ask? *Dios,* Leila. You've been on the island how long?'

'I swear to you—I was trying to choose the right moment, and I thought I'd found it. I was coming to find you, but then I saw the stall selling baby clothes and I was distracted. I couldn't resist—'

She stopped and her eyes filled with tears. He knew then that the tiny clothes were innocent reminders to Leila of the small child who would wear them and as such they were more than baby clothes, they were Leila's promise of the future. He wanted to embrace her, to tell her it would be all right, but, unlike Leila, the thought of an impending birth filled him with dread. He had the additional concern of being responsible for a child when his own father had ruined so many lives, and, even if he could do better, how could he balance his responsibilities of running a multinational corporation with being a father?

'I've handled this badly,' he admitted. 'I keep things simple so I don't end up with children who are farmed out to their grandparents, because their parents have better things to do.'

'Is that what happened to you, Raffa?'

He could do without the compassion on her face. He didn't need anyone's pity, and, with an impatient gesture, he turned away.

'You already told me that your grandmother brought you up—'

'And made a damn good job of it,' he said quietly.

'So your parents didn't want children—'

'Please,' he said. 'Please stop before you make things worse.'

'You'll see,' she said confidently. 'In a few months' time our baby will be here and you'll feel differently.'

The irony of their role reversal struck him, as Leila, speaking with such confidence about the birth, left him racked with fear for her. She couldn't know what lay ahead of her, and this new Leila was frightened of nothing and no one—would listen to no one, not even him.

'I'm only concerned for your safety, and for the baby's safety,' he assured her. 'But if you want to hear that I'm the by-product of too much sex and too little love, then you would be right.'

'So where does that leave us, Raffa?'

'All you need to know is that love was never a factor. Not once. Not ever—'

He was still back in the past, talking about his parents, but then he noticed that Leila's face had turned ashen. She thought he was talking about them.

'Well, if nothing else,' she said gamely, 'I understand you better now.'

He should have known she would find some good amongst the debris. As the ghosts bore down on him he shook his head. 'I doubt that somehow.'

The mother he'd never known was dead. And his father—a man he hadn't spoken to for years—was currently sunning himself with the latest in a long line of teenage girlfriends in Monte Carlo. His grandmother had saved him, and it was Abuelita who had restored his faith in human nature.

Leila put her hand on his arm, and he was sure they both felt the shock of the physical contact. 'I should have found some better way to tell you,' she said. 'But at least you know now. Perhaps it would be better for all concerned if things are handled formally between us by a third party as you suggested. I'll return home as soon as you can make arrangements for me to leave.'

No, was his first reaction. She couldn't leave. For a whole raft of reasons, not least of which was Leila herself, fast followed by his concern over the birth of her child. There must have been something of this in his eyes as he turned to look at her, and she lifted her hand as if to ward him off. Moving her hand aside, he dragged her close.

'Don't do this, Raffa. Please…'

She knew it was hopeless to resist just as he did. The passion between them was so easily ignited and it had been far too long for both of them. As Leila reached up to link her hands behind his neck, he kissed her hungrily, and, lifting her into his arms, he carried her across the hallway and up the stairs into his apartment. Kicking the door shut behind him, he crossed the room and laid her down on the bed. Undoing the buckle on his jeans, he lowered the zipper and freed himself. Lifting Leila's skirt, he dispensed with her thong and settled over her. Driving a thigh between her legs—

He stopped.

Massively erect and hideously frustrated, he stopped. Pulling back, he swung off the bed.

'What?' she said, reaching for him.

'I can't do this, Leila.' Raking stiff fingers through his hair, he asked himself, what had he become? And then he swung round to find Leila crying.

Dios! What a mess this was.

CHAPTER SEVEN

LEILA CRYING SHAMED HIM. She wasn't the type to use tears as a weapon, or even as a last resort. Leila had never been quiet and ineffective. She possessed an inner strength. Even now she wasn't making a fuss as she straightened her clothes with a gentle grace that made him feel more of a brute than ever.

'Thank you,' she whispered, sensing his gaze on her.

'What the hell are you thanking me for?'

'You stopped,' she said as if that were obvious. 'You knew when to stop.' She looked up at him. 'And you could stop, Raffa.'

'Of course I could stop.' He frowned. 'I can't imagine why that should surprise you.'

Unless...

'Perhaps we both have issues from the past we're still working through,' she said, confirming his worst suspicions. 'I wanted you with a madness that drove everything else from my mind, and I think you wanted me.'

'You only think?'

'But you realised it wasn't the right time for either of us, and so you stopped.'

'Of course I stopped.' He shook his head, trying to make sense of something that made no sense. He lifted his shoulders in a shrug. 'I had to stop.'

His world might be very different from Leila's, according to her, but trust between a man and a woman when they were having sex was a given. He wondered now what she was hiding, and suddenly he dreaded hearing her answer to the question he had to ask. 'Have you been assaulted, Leila?'

'No.'

She spoke so quickly he believed her, but there was still a haunted look in her eyes.

'But there is something?'

He waited, but she said nothing more.

'I would never hurt you. I hope you know that.'

She didn't answer. She wasn't ready to talk to him yet. He knew something of Leila's family history from the press reports, and now his imagination was working overtime. The thought of what she might have seen at home chilled him. 'Can you tell me what's wrong?' he pressed gently.

'Not now, Raffa.'

She would tell him, he hoped, but it would be in her own time. 'Will you be all right in here if I leave you for a while?' He sensed she needed space; he did too.

'Of course I'll be all right, Raffa.'

There was such a mix of emotion in her eyes when she looked up at him, he guessed neither of them had an answer for the heat that had flared between them.

'Come and find me when you're ready,' he suggested. 'Have a rest—or don't have a rest. Do whatever you think best.'

'Thank you. I will,' she assured him quietly.

She waited until all the rattling atoms in the room had settled like dust, and then, standing up, she brushed herself down as if brushing away the ghosts of the past. It was time to tell Raffa everything. She wanted to help him, and if she confided in him perhaps they could re-build their trust. It was time to open up in the hope that he would do the same.

She guessed she'd find him in the courtyard. He was chatting with some of the older men who had come along to help him organise the fair. Sensing her arrival, he turned to look at her long before she reached him.

'Good—you're here,' he said. 'Let's go for that walk.' He introduced her and then explained their intentions in Spanish to the group of elderly men, who smiled broadly at her and, like everyone else on the island, instantly made her feel a very welcome part of their community.

'The gardens?' Raffa suggested as he escorted her through the line of stalls.

'Perfect,' Leila agreed.

The gardens surrounding the castle were ordered and tranquil, and she couldn't think of anywhere better to say the words she had never shared with anyone, not even her sisters or her brother, Tyr.

The scent of the recently watered grass combined with the heady scent of the roses in the flower beds was both intoxicating and soothing, and when they stopped beside a fountain she dabbled her fingertips in the cool-ing pool.

'My father beat my mother. Not once, but many times.' Her voice was flat, devoid of expression.

'*Dios,* Leila.'

'My mother knew I'd seen what had happened,' she continued without looking at Raffa. 'It was our unspo-ken pact. We both knew my father would never dare to touch her in front of my sisters, let alone in front of Tyr. She explained away the bumps and bruises as her own clumsy fault. I suppose that's why my mother's last wish was that I didn't live scared because of what I'd seen.'

Gathering Leila into his arms, he held her close. 'You are strong,' he whispered fiercely against her hair. 'Your mother would be proud of you, Leila. You're stronger than you know.'

'How can that be when I've done everything wrong?' she whispered.

'What have you done wrong?' he demanded, pulling back to look at her.

'I tried to become the woman my mother always wanted me to be, and look what a mess I've made of everything. I should have told you about the baby the instant I knew.'

'If you could have found me,' he reminded her. 'I'm good at disappearing.'

'Like my brother, Tyr,' she mused.

His loyalty to Tyr made him ignore that comment. 'And as far as dealing with the ghosts of the past is concerned, I'd say you've coped a lot better than I have.'

'What do you mean by that, Raffa?'

He shrugged it off. 'Whatever else this baby means to you, Leila, it can't form part of your self-improvement plan.'

'That's just it. I never planned to have a baby with you, Raffa. I never sleep around. I never have. And I certainly wouldn't use you to have a baby.'

'But now you are pregnant I must help you.' His heart lurched at the thought that Leila might say no. His plans to control every aspect of this birth were already taking shape in his mind.

'Don't look so haunted, Raffa. I'm healthy and I'm young, and I'll do everything I can to give our child the best possible start in life.'

'You have to allow me to worry about you. I always plan ahead, but still things can go wrong.'

'Nothing's going to go wrong, Raffa.'

As far as she knew. He was prepared to cut Leila all the slack in the world after what she'd told him, and he would try his best to calm his raging concern where the actual birth of the baby was concerned, but, where Leila's life and the life of their unborn child was concerned, he refused to take any chances.

'So what's your solution, Raffa?'

'We take things one step at a time. I'll have my doctors check you over and then we can move forward with more confidence to the next stage.'

She flashed him a reproachful glance. 'You mean you want your doctor to make sure it's your baby?'

'No. My only concern is that you and the baby are healthy, Leila. I'm suggesting you have a scan, to establish how far the pregnancy has progressed, so you know that everything's progressing normally.'

'You should be there for the first scan. A friend showed me a picture once. It's…' She stopped and smiled at him. 'There are no words.' Leila's face was rapt.

'That may not be possible. I have…commitments.' Commitments he couldn't discuss with Tyr's sister.

'Oh,' she said softly, masking her bitter disappointment behind a brave face and a determined chin.

'And we have to decide where you'll live,' he said, moving on.

'In Skavanga, of course.' She frowned.

'With my child? So I can look forward to seeing my son or daughter—what? Every six weeks or so?'

She couldn't meet his gaze.

'I don't think so, Leila. When we have a clearer

picture of when the baby's due, I'll draw up a visitation plan—'

'You'll draw it up?'

'In consultation with you.'

'You make it sound so cold. You can't just drive through what suits you best, Raffa. I'll take care of our child, and not with you looking over my shoulder to see if you approve.'

'And how will you do that on the salary you currently earn?'

'I have shares in the mine and, when your consortium has completed its investment and everything is running at full capacity, I've been led to believe I should be paid a healthy dividend.'

'You will benefit,' he agreed, 'but not enough. You're a very small shareholder, and my child—'

'Ah,' she interrupted. 'So now we come to it. Any child of yours will have different needs from every other child in the world. If it's a boy it will inherit a dukedom, and either sex will inherit a fortune. Where I come from, love and food and warmth and safety are the primary requirements for a child.'

'That's where we differ, Leila, because I don't see any separation between me and the rest of the world.'

'Just a few billion.'

'That doesn't make me special. I got lucky, that's all.'

'And you work hard,' Leila remarked in her equal-handed way.

'Yes, I do, and I don't want you working all the hours God sends in order to support our baby. This is my responsibility too. I'm just trying to make things easier for you, Leila.'

'But you live in such a different world.'

'It's warmer,' he agreed wryly.

'You know what I mean,' she insisted, but thankfully he had succeeded in lightening the atmosphere, and now she was trying not to smile.

'As far as I'm concerned, we live in the same world, Leila. You want to work. I want to work. If a child enters my life I want that child to enjoy the benefits I can provide for it. Otherwise, what the hell am I working for?'

If he could brush aside his fears for Leila for only a second he could see that with a child in his life there would be real purpose to the drive that carried him forward so relentlessly. He worked to help others, but to be able to do that and have a child of his own to do things for...

'I would never stop you seeing the baby, Raffa.'

He refocused on Leila's face, wondering what had prompted that remark. 'Custody is a long way from being decided yet.'

'But a child should live with its mother—'

'Don't you trust me, Leila?'

'Yes...'

No, he thought as she fell silent. Leila didn't trust him with something as precious as her child. Why should she when she hardly knew him? Leila only wanted to be a good mother. She would never forget that her own mother had been killed so tragically when she was so young, or what a sense of loss she had felt since then.

'We'll decide this together. Perhaps we should continue this discussion when you're feeling less emotional.'

'In around a couple of years' time?' she suggested, her amused glance flashing up to meet his.

'Whenever you're ready,' he said gently.

There was a long silence and then she said, 'I think I'm always going to be influenced by the letter my mother wrote to me before she died. I think she was trying to prepare me for the big things in life, like this.'

'A letter?'

'I had to promise to be bold...take life by the scruff of the neck and forge my own path, rather than allowing the past to haunt me and hold me back.' She smiled. 'I was trying to get the balance right and went overboard on the night of the party.'

They both had, he remembered, thinking back. Before that night he guessed Leila had made do with dreams, because dreams were safe and available to everyone, even the quietest of sisters. 'We will work this out, Leila, and while we do there's something you could do for me.'

She looked at him and raised a brow. 'What could I possibly do for you, Raffa?'

His grandmother's illness had really thrown him. Leila's news had really thrown him. Perhaps if he brought the two of them together... 'There's someone I'd like you to meet.'

'Who?' she said suspiciously.

'My grandmother. You did say you'd like to meet her.'

'I would. But how does that help our situation?'

'I don't know. Maybe it won't,' he admitted. 'But I think we should tell her you're expecting her first great-grandchild, don't you?'

CHAPTER EIGHT

RAFFA WANTED TO introduce her to the matriarch of his family? Maybe he was right and she was blinkered. Seeing herself as the small-town girl and Raffa as somehow inhabiting a different world was blown to smithereens when he had exactly the same concerns she had: family, and the people who depended on him.

'But what can I tell your grandmother?' The last thing she wanted was to upset an old lady who had been sick recently. 'I'm pregnant with your child, but I'm going home to Skavanga, so she may never see her great-grandchild. Perhaps it's better if we don't meet.'

'I won't force you to meet her.'

'Your grandmother has been ill and I can't imagine that meeting me is going to make her feel better.'

'You'd be surprised.' A glint of amusement brightened his eyes. 'You'd give her hope.'

'I don't see how.'

'She's given up on me becoming any type of family man.'

'So you parade me in front of her? How's that going to work? I don't doubt your grandmother longs for you to settle down and give her a great-grandchild, but please leave me out of it.'

'I would never attempt to mislead my grandmother. I would tell her the truth as I always do.'

'That's sure to cheer her up.'

'It's better than nothing.'

A flicker of humour crept into Leila's gaze. 'I don't think you know the first thing about women, Raffa.'

Raffa drew back his head in surprise. No doubt he considered himself an expert on women.

'Introducing the mother of my child to my grandmother is the right thing to do,' he said stiffly.

'And I'd love to meet her,' Leila confirmed, 'but I refuse to suggest that our relationship is anything more than it is.' That was a platonic working relationship between two people who just happened to be expecting a child.

As Raffa inclined his head in agreement she knew she'd have to watch him. Raffa Leon was used to having everything his own way, and for once in his life he would have to accept that that wasn't going to happen this time.

Raffa's grandmother's house wasn't close to the castle, as Leila had imagined, but about an hour's drive away, up in the hills where it was cooler. Raffa drove them up the switchback road in an open-topped bright red Maserati, and, apart from the thrill of riding in a sports car with a man who knew what he was doing, the view over a vine-crammed valley on one side, and a neon-bright sea on the other, went a long way to soothing her tension at the thought of finally meeting his grandmother.

It was a lovely day, with a breeze laden with the scent of blossom, and would have been a perfect day had it not been for the man at her side making her jittery. Raffa was wound up like a spring. This visit clearly meant a lot to him. The excess energy he was burning was as potent as any aphrodisiac, which was inconvenient on a day when her aim was to appear strait-laced and sensible, the type of girl who might make a mistake once in the heat of the moment, but who would never make the same mistake twice.

'My grandmother appreciates her own space,' Raffa explained as he turned off the main road onto an impressive tree-lined drive.

'And who could blame your grandmother for wanting to get away from you?' Leila said dryly. 'Or for wanting to live here?' she breathed, taking in the magnificent surroundings.

The picturesque drive boasted a shady avenue of lush green trees that led the way to a quaint sprawling manor house built of stone. With a cheery red front door and dozens of mullioned windows twinkling a welcome, the picture-postcard setting was made complete by a chorus line of colourful songbirds perched on the gabled roof. The manor house was one of the prettiest buildings Leila had ever seen, and was set off to perfection by the banks of flower beds in front of it, and the spray of cooling fountains in the yard.

'It's like a fairy dell,' she said, glancing around.

'My grandmother works hard on the gardens, but so far no sighting of fairies.' Pushing his sunglasses back on his head, Raffa opened the car door for her with a slanting smile.

'Just before we go in…' Leila turned to face Raffa beneath a porch extravagantly swagged with peach-coloured wisteria. 'What exactly have you told your grandmother about us?'

'That I'm bringing a very good friend to meet her. That is what we agreed, isn't it?'

She confirmed this tensely with a nod. She wouldn't

have believed it possible for any woman to have a platonic friendship with Raffa Leon, so it appeared she had achieved the impossible.

Wearing jeans and a tight-fitting top that clung to his sculpted muscles with loving attention to detail, rugged, too handsome for his own good, Raffa exuded raw, animal sex, and it was impossible to stand this close to him without imagining being intimate with him. It didn't help that she had some rather compelling memories to draw on.

'You look fine,' he said as she fiddled with her dress.

She'd chosen it carefully, thinking Raffa's grandmother had enough to contend with today without a fashion crisis hitting her between the eyes. It was a pretty dress with a floral pattern, a respectable neckline and a knee-length skirt.

'My grandmother speaks fluent English, though no Scandinavian languages,' Raffa explained, 'but as you're both fluent in English...'

'We'll be fine.'

Raffa was such a distraction she was careful not to look at him and it was a relief to hear footsteps inside the house coming closer. There was one brief moment when her concentration lapsed as Raffa eased onto one hip and her pulse jagged, but she quickly turned her thoughts to meeting his grandmother and everything settled down again.

The housekeeper's welcome was warm. Her apple cheeks were split by a wide smile as she embraced Raffa, proving he was clearly a popular visitor. The rest of the staff seemed excited by his arrival as they walked through the exquisitely furnished house, and Leila was conscious of attracting quite a bit of interest too.

'The dowager duchess is in the garden,' the housekeeper explained as she led them through a light-filled orangery.

The dowager duchess. Leila's heart began to pound. The title alone made Raffa's grandmother sound quite formidable.

Far from being a grande dame, as Leila had feared, the dowager duchess turned out to be a dainty, bird-like woman, with silver hair twisted into a casual bun on top of her head with a moth-eaten straw hat crammed on top of it. Wiry and upright, she was dressed in wide-legged linen trousers and a serviceable, long-sleeved blouse. A multi-pocketed gardening apron in a nondescript dun colour, out of which protruded an assortment of stakes, recent snippings and secateurs, completed her outfit. She was very much in charge of a squad of gardeners, whom she was directing as briskly as a sergeant major around her park-sized garden.

Leila only had to glance at Raffa to know how he felt about this woman. They adored each other, she realised, standing back as the giant of a man and the tiny woman embraced each other. When Raffa stood back to introduce her, she discovered that his grandmother had been well briefed in advance of her arrival.

'I hear congratulations are in order,' she exclaimed, drawing Leila into a hug. 'I'm so happy for both of you.'

Leila's gaze found Raffa's, and she wondered now if he'd told his grandmother some cock-and-bull story regarding their relationship.

He shrugged and his eyes were full of amusement as if to prove that Raffa Leon answered to no one.

'Come with me, Leila,' his grandmother invited warmly, unaware of the tension between her grandson and her guest. 'We'll have tea in the garden. I think

Rafael has got your message,' she added with amusement. 'You have the most expressive eyes.'

'I'm sorry if I've offended you,' Leila said as they sat down.

'Please don't apologise. I know Rafael, and I always make up my own mind, whatever he tells me.'

A table draped with a delicate lace cloth and an array of fine china had been set out for them beneath the generous shade of an ancient frangipani tree. Following Leila's glance across the manicured lawn as Raffa headed back to the house, his grandmother leaned forward to remark, 'Don't look so worried, Leila. The Dukes of Cantalabria have always been notoriously unscrupulous when it comes to choosing a bride.'

'A bride?' No amount of good manners could hide Leila's feelings. 'I'm not sure what Raffa has told you, but I've no intention of marrying him.'

'Of course not. Please forgive me. Seeing the two of you together takes me back to my own youth.'

'I'm afraid ours is not a lasting relationship.'

'With a child between you?' the dowager queried. 'I'd say there's a lifetime's commitment between you. Milk or lemon, my dear?'

'Lemon, please.' Leila's voice took on a new intensity. 'I just don't want to mislead you in any way.'

'How are you misleading me?' The old lady frowned as she passed Leila a delicate porcelain cup and saucer. 'Any fool can see my grandson is head over heels in love with you.'

Leila almost laughed out loud, but, in deference to Raffa's grandmother, she killed the impulse in favour of being frank with her. 'Raffa's not in love with me. All we shared was a moment of—'

'Pure passion,' his grandmother supplied with a nod

of her head. 'Don't look so surprised, Leila. I was young once. And please...I don't want you to feel awkward around me. I can assure you, it would take a lot more than your pregnancy to shock me. I'm only surprised Rafael can be so calm about it.'

'Calm?' Leila tensed.

The old lady started as if she had been jolted out of revisiting memories from the past.

'Forgive me, Leila. I knew this day would come. I just wasn't sure how Rafael would cope with it. It's great credit to you that he's taken it so calmly. I'm delighted for him—for both of you.'

Far from being reassured, Leila was doubly anxious, and determined to get to the bottom of Raffa's mysterious past. 'Is there some family problem I should know about?'

'You're thinking genetic problems,' the dowager observed shrewdly. 'Let me reassure you right away, it's nothing like that, Leila. I'm thrilled you're having a child, and there's no reason to suppose your baby won't be perfectly healthy.'

'But is there something more I should know?'

'What *do* you know?' The dowager stared at her levelly.

'Only a little,' Leila admitted, hoping the old lady would fill in the gaps.

'Drink your tea before it gets cold, dear,' the dowager said, dashing Leila's hopes.

'I'm glad I've had this chance to meet you,' Leila said to break the sudden silence. 'It meant a lot to Raffa.'

'And I'm delighted to meet the mother of my first great-grandchild.' There was a pause, and then the dowager covered Leila's hand with hers. 'Forgive me, Leila, but there are things that cannot be discussed over tea. I'm sure Raffa will explain.'

'Yes. I'm sure he will,' Leila agreed without much conviction, her anxiety levels rising by the minute as she wondered what Raffa's grandmother could mean.

'How long are you staying?' The dowager's shrewd gaze met Leila's over their teacups.

'Not long,' Leila said honestly. 'Just long enough to choose some gems to display in Skavanga.'

'At the museum you're in control of,' the dowager said with interest, putting down her cup. 'Perhaps I'll pay you a visit one day. Now where is my grandson?' she said, turning in her chair. 'Perhaps he's choosing some gems to show you. We keep some of the very best in an armed vault in the house,' she added with a touch of the familiar family steel.

Leila's tension eased into a smile. 'You are so like Raffa.'

'Stubborn? Driven?' the old lady suggested, meeting Leila's gaze. There was a twinkle in her eye as she leaned forward. 'Fiercely determined to have our own way? Something tells me you're just like us, Leila Skavanga.'

CHAPTER NINE

'TALK OF THE DEVIL!' the dowager exclaimed as Raffa appeared in the doorway of the house.

The mellow sunshine and the beautiful garden provided a deceptively soft frame for a hard man. A hard man with a mysterious past, Leila now knew, determined she would get to the bottom of the mystery.

Would she always feel this way when she saw him? Leila wondered as Raffa strode towards them. Yes, she realised as he flashed a quick smile. And this was her chance, maybe her only chance to find out what his grandmother had meant when she talked about Raffa's concerns regarding Leila's pregnancy. As soon as he was within earshot she sprang up. 'Could we have a walk round your beautiful garden?' she asked the dowager.

'Of course. Rafael, please escort our guest.'

The heady scent of the flowers was intoxicating, but that was nothing compared to standing close to Raffa, only inches away...feeling his gaze on her back as she bent down to smell the roses, or feeling his breath brush her neck when she straightened up.

'So, what's this about?' he said as they walked towards a small bridge across the stream that ran through the garden. 'What did you want to talk about that you can't say in front of my grandmother?'

Pausing in the middle of the bridge, Leila leaned back against the worn balustrade with her arms resting on the warm, smooth wood. 'Your grandmother said she was surprised that you could take my pregnancy so calmly. She said there were things it wasn't possible to discuss over tea. She reassured me that there were no genetic problems in your family to worry about, so I wondered—'

'My grandmother said too much.'

He hadn't meant to snap. Or turn his back. Or lean over the bridge lost in his thought, but the guilt he had lived with for so long was curdling inside him. He had to take several deep breaths before he could control the emotion. Feelings that had been buried for so long had a way of running wild. They had threatened to ruin him as a youth, but he had mastered them as an adult, and control ruled him now. Leila must think him distant and aloof from her, but she was wrong. He was intensely focused on the only thing that mattered to him now, which was Leila's safety when she gave birth to their child.

'Raffa?'

'What?'

'Have I said something to upset you? I didn't mean to be intrusive or to probe into your past.'

'I know.' He still didn't turn around. It would have been easier for both of them if he had kept Leila at a distance, stopped her coming to the island, but his head had been full of her, and he doubted now that any amount of work or distraction could shake her out. He couldn't have known she was carrying his baby, or how that would make him feel. He could never have anticipated the old ghosts from the past coming back to taunt him with the guilt he'd lived with all his life.

Following Raffa's gaze down the busy stream as it

rushed and bubbled on its way to the sea, she could feel the barricades rising around him. Raffa's self-imposed isolation was a shield to keep her and the world at bay, and whatever had made Raffa withdraw into himself, it was something he had kept hidden for years, so he was hardly going to blurt it out now. But her impulse was to reassure him, and there was nothing to stop her doing that.

'Your grandmother cares very much about you, Raffa. She didn't break any confidences. She wouldn't tell me anything.'

Straightening up, he turned to face her, and his expression had not mellowed as she'd hoped. 'Is that what this walk is about?' There was suspicion in his voice, even hostility. 'Do you expect me to reveal all now?'

'No,' she said, holding Raffa's burning gaze steadily. 'Of course I don't. I just wanted you to know you're not alone.'

'It's you we're supposed to be sorting out, Leila.'

'I don't need sorting out. And you shouldn't be so proud that you can't admit that you do.'

'What?' he said softly.

'I'm sorry, but someone has to tell you. Your grandmother is one of the strongest women I've ever met, but she loves you so much she has spent her whole life tiptoeing around you, and whatever it is that makes you feel so guilty. And I won't do that.'

Drawing back his head, Raffa stared down at her in disbelief.

Even now, even with Raffa glowering down at her, her only wish was to reach out to him and hold him until the ghosts had no strength left. He was a pent-up powerhouse of outraged affront, which increased the force of his physical appeal tenfold. She felt it as a primitive and very earthy response to him, and Raffa felt it too. Just the smallest change in those hostile dark eyes told her exactly how Raffa Leon would like to resolve this situation. Perhaps the combined force of their passion would be enough to banish all their ghosts in one fell swoop, she reflected wryly.

'Shall we say goodbye to my grandmother?' Raffa suggested in a neutral tone.

'Yes,' she agreed in the same careful manner.

'Seat belt,' Raffa reminded her as they slid into the car.

Before she could reach for it, he had leaned across to help and his considerable weight pressed against her breasts. The catch clicked into place and still they remained motionless. Glancing into Raffa's eyes, she saw the heat in them and felt an answering tug.

Settling back into the driver's seat, he reached for his sunglasses and switched on the engine, by which time the aching need inside her had grown to a pulsing urge to mate. Would she ever find an answer to her obsession with this man?

Her life had changed completely since meeting Raffa. She had changed completely, Leila realised as he gunned the engine and released the brake. She glanced at Raffa's harsh profile, and then on to assess his impossibly powerful frame like a trainer at the stockyard picking out the king of the herd, a magnificent wild stallion to mount, to tame, to ride.

If that was all that lay behind the attraction, perhaps she could forget her principles for one day, slake her lust and go home, but there was so much more to Raffa Leon. She was compelled to stay so she could enjoy more of his passion, his humour and his whip-sharp mind, and uncover all those secrets his grandmother had hinted at.

She had never been a quitter, Leila reflected as Raffa floored the accelerator and G-force thumped her in the back.

He drove the car to its limits. There was something hot about a woman carrying his child that made Leila irresistible. He had to have her right away. She was sending him all the same messages and he was drowning in pheromones. He could never have anticipated the way Leila's pregnancy would make him feel—protective, yes, possessive too, but in a good way, a way that made him want to stake his claim over and over, so he could hear her cries of pleasure.

'What are you smiling at?' she asked him.

'Am I?' he retorted innocently. He was remembering the way she'd stood up to him—challenged him. He couldn't remember anyone doing that. Leila was right about his grandmother tiptoeing around him, but it wasn't just his grandmother who did that. When it came to his past, no one trespassed. But Leila had, and, though she had jolted him out of the status quo, it only made him think more of her. There was nothing weak about Leila beneath that peacemaking manner, and he liked that.

The visit with his grandmother had been a success. He had hoped they would like each other. He just hadn't realised how much. With his *abuelita* as an ally Leila had no reason not to stay on the island to have her baby. He had already appointed her doctors, and the support staff was on standby. Leila might have amused him by standing up to him, but control over this birth was all his.

'Why are we stopping?' she said as he pulled off the road.

'We're stopping because some things can't wait.'

'Like what?' she said, her voice shaking with excitement as she feigned innocence and gazed around.

'Like the view is spectacular?' He raised a brow. The view was spectacular, but they both knew that wasn't the reason he'd stopped the car.

'You can't,' she protested when he removed his seat belt. 'Raffa—what if someone drives past?'

'So that isn't a flat no?' he said, curbing a smile. 'You have an urge. I have an urge. Let's do something about it.'

'How do you know I have got an urge?'

'Your eyes are darkening… Your lips are swelling… Your nipples are—'

'Stop,' she said, sucking in a fast breath. 'You are so bad.'

'Would you have me any other way?' As he angled his chin he saw the answer in her eyes. Reaching across, he very gently stroked the swell of her belly and a sigh escaped her.

'You're a very bad man, Raffa Leon.'

'I make you angry?'

'Yes, you do.'

'Then please allow me to soothe you,' he suggested, tipping his sunglasses down his nose. Drawing her into his arms, he lazily brushed her lips with his.

She was only wearing a tiny thong beneath the dress. No bra. She didn't need one. Her breasts were glorious, firm and full, while her nipples were engorged and pressing urgently against the fine, summer-weight fabric, in serious danger of being chafed unless he freed them.

'What are you doing?' she demanded in a husky whisper.

'Feeding,' he growled, laving her nipples with his tongue. 'Hmm. You taste different.'

'Soapy?' she suggested.

'No. Womanly and—'

'Pregnant?'

'Maybe.' He gave a crooked smile as he gazed up into Leila's eyes.

'No maybe about it,' she said, breaking off to gasp when his hand stroked her thigh.

'Nice?' he asked, trailing his fingertips over her.

Leila's answer was to arc towards him, making herself more available. 'Not sure I can bear being teased,' she warned him. 'Being pregnant seems to have made me...'

'Mad for sex.'

'How do you know?'

'I know everything about you, Leila Skavanga. And it's been far too long.'

Removing her thong, he slipped down from his seat and went to kneel in the well of the car. 'Rest your legs on my shoulders and your feet on the dashboard.'

'Really?' she said, glancing around.

'Really,' he confirmed.

'How do I explain this if a tractor drives past?' she managed between hectic breaths.

'Just say you've got a cramp and I'm doing the best I can to distract you—'

'In Spanish?'

He grinned as he freed himself with one hand and positioned her with the other.

'Don't stop,' she begged him when he got busy with his tongue. 'Don't you dare stop... Oh, this is so good...'

He teased her again with just a fraction of his length.

'I want all of it,' she insisted.

'Greedy must wait—'

'Who says?' she demanded, thrusting forward.

It was his turn to groan. She was so tight, so hot and wet, and such an unbelievably perfect fit for him. And this was a really great position. Leila was at the perfect height for him so all he had to do was rock back and forth. It felt so good, so necessary, and it was only a matter of moments before they both lost it.

'Again,' she demanded, still pulsing round him.

Leila hadn't been joking when she said she was mad for sex, but then they'd always been mad for each other. There was some special chemistry between them that reason had never played a part in. 'I think you like that,' he murmured as she groaned.

Leila's answer was to grip him with her internal muscles and tell him fiercely, 'I love it!'

Binding his buttocks close with fingers of steel, she rubbed herself against him until he was almost in danger of losing control, and it was only when they heard the sound of an engine in the distance that they stopped. He tried to find Leila's thong, but a search under the seats proved futile and he was forced to give up.

'The heat between us must have vaporised it,' she said, trying not to laugh.

He secured their seat belts and they sat bolt upright, looking respectable just in time for the local bus to drive past.

'Well, that must have been quite a shock for them,' Leila said, whipping her thong off the dashboard, where it had been all this time. 'I guess our secret is out.'

'Looks like it,' he agreed, looping his arm around her neck to drag her close for a kiss.

Resting his forehead against Leila's, he wanted this moment to last. Maybe this could work. Maybe he could persuade Leila that there would be benefits beyond her imagining if she agreed to live in Spain with their child.

'Do you always get your own way?' she murmured against his mouth as if reading his thoughts.

'Always,' he said confidently.

'Then I think you might just have to get used to me saying no, Raffa Leon, because I can be difficult—and stubborn. Just ask my sisters.'

Unconcerned, he reached across, and, lifting her into his arms, he positioned Leila on his lap. 'Say no,' he invited.

CHAPTER TEN

THINGS HAPPENED FAST in his world and even faster in Leila's, it turned out. He had left Leila on the island for a brief twenty-four hours to attend a meeting in London, and by the time he got back she had introduced herself to his staff, drawn up a schedule of training visits to help improve her insight of the retail diamond industry and booked an appointment with her own doctor in Skavanga.

'You'll go to my doctor, Leila.'

'Don't you trust me to handle this, Raffa?' She didn't even trouble to raise her head from the latest academic paper on heat treatment of gemstones she was reading.

'I have engaged the foremost obstetrician to guide you through this birth. If he's good enough for the British royal family, he should be good enough for you.'

She gave him a direct look over the top of the cute little spectacles she wore for close work. 'And I have arranged to speak to my family doctor, a woman who has known me all my life. I don't need the foremost man,' she added. 'Birth is a natural process, Raffa. I'm not ill. I'm pregnant.'

'You'll do as I say.'

'Really?' she said mildly. Standing up to confront

him, she added, 'I think you'll find that this is my body, my baby and my decision to make.'

'This is our baby and I won't take any chances with either of you.'

As Leila stabbed a look at him he reined back. She was sitting on top of a hormonal volcano. He should remember that.

'You're going to be a father, Raffa.'

Yes. He was going to be a father...

He tried to feel something.

He felt nothing but the customary throb of anxiety. He envied the contented smile on Leila's lips. Knowing she was going to be a mother had lit her up from the inside out, while all he could do was dread the birth.

'No,' he argued flatly, forgetting everything he had vowed to do and say. 'You will not be having your baby in Skavanga. You will have your baby here on the island, where I can keep you safe.'

'But I've never suggested anything different other than having my baby in Skavanga,' Leila protested, frowning as she looked at him as if he'd gone mad. 'I can't understand why you're making such a fuss about it. We have a state-of-the-art hospital in Skavanga and excellent specialists, most of whom I know.'

'I have no doubt that you have every confidence in them,' he said, 'but I have appointed the best.'

'Oh,' she mocked him. 'I forgot for a moment that your money can buy anything, including guaranteed, trouble-free birth.'

He swung away so she couldn't see the expression on his face. 'It can provide a substantial buffer against any unpleasantness for you,' he said, turning slowly round to face her. 'And yes, in my experience, my money does buy the best.'

'But it can't buy me, or my agreement to your plan. Are you seriously suggesting a doctor who has known me all my life would let me come to any harm?' she pressed him.

He shook his head. 'I'm not prepared to take that risk.' This wasn't up for discussion.

'Well, I'm not going to London,' she said, holding his stare unblinking.

'Did I say anything about London?'

She frowned. 'No, but I thought—'

'You'll stay here on the island. The specialist and his team will come to you. You'll have the finest midwife, nurses, and a paediatrician especially appointed for the baby. And as far as the accessories are concerned, you can order anything you want online.'

'The accessories,' she echoed as if mystified. 'You make our baby sound like this season's fashion must-have.'

'Don't be so ridiculous, Leila.'

'But you don't show any more involvement than that, Raffa.' Leila's face was tense with disappointment.

'Imagine having a nursery at the castle,' he pressed on. 'I know how much you loved your turret room, and you can speak to my decorators, have the nursery decked out any way you want. The top stores will provide cribs and toys and clothes and strollers, and any other baby equipment you might need. You'll have a completely free hand, Leila—'

'But I'll be a prisoner,' she said with horror.

He shook his head wryly. 'I thought we'd got past that Rapunzel thing. You'll be free to come and go as you like.'

'After the birth.'

'Well, obviously.'

As he gazed around the room Leila had been using as an office he should have known that a carefully preserved sixteenth-century citadel with a sheikh's ransom in antiques and furnishings would cut no ice with her. He was right. Those hormones hadn't gone anywhere; they were merely slumbering, waiting to explode.

'You can't keep me trapped on your island when I want to go home.'

'Just think carefully before you make any rash decisions. Think about what you want, and then think about what's best for the baby.'

'Don't patronise me, Raffa,' she said quietly. 'I don't need to think about what's best for my baby. What's best for both of us is for me to return home to Skavanga and my life there.'

'I'm not trying to patronise you. I'm trying to do everything I can to help you.'

'Then let me go.'

Her voice was barely above a whisper, but the expression in her eyes as she held his gaze was absolutely determined.

'At least agree to sleep on it.'

She stood up, ready to go. 'I will,' she promised without much enthusiasm.

By this time they were mere inches apart. 'What are you doing?' she said.

'I'm kissing you into compliance.' Brushing her lips with his mouth to a lazy rhythm he felt her soften in his arms.

'Get off me,' she warned, starting to laugh as he continued to tease her. 'You can't get around me like this.'

'Can't I?' His hands had moved down to cup the swell

of her buttocks, bringing Leila into contact with the best argument he'd got.

'You're unscrupulous.'

'Yes, I am,' he agreed.

'And a very bad man,' she added with a shuddering sigh.

'We've already established that,' he confirmed, rasping the tender skin below her ear very lightly with his stubble. 'Shall we continue this discussion in the morning?'

'I'm not going to change my mind,' she insisted, turning to stare into his eyes.

But she wasn't going to discourage Raffa from trying his absolute best to convince her he was right either, Leila concluded as he swung her into his arms.

Raffa shouldered the door to his bedroom and carried her inside, kissing her across the room before lowering her gently onto the bed, where he stripped off her dress and tossed it aside. As it floated to the floor she remembered the incident with the thong, and warned him not to lose her dress. 'I don't want to walk through the castle naked to find it.'

'These walls must have seen a lot of excitement in their time. Perhaps I should send the staff home and let you do just that.'

'Then you should strip off too,' she insisted. 'Why don't I help you?'

She lingered over every glorious inch of him, peeling back his top slowly so she could appreciate the bronze map of hard muscle…the flat stomach…the impossible width of his shoulders, tapering down to the washboard waist—

'Let me help you,' Raffa offered when she fumbled with his belt.

Swinging off the bed, he freed the tine. His jeans and boxers followed, and she was glad of her ringside seat as Raffa turned his back to stretch like a big cat. Every inch of him was bronze, and his thighs were towers of muscle, his legs so lean and long. His calves were powerful, and even his naked feet were sexy. She loved his naked feet. But most of all she loved his hard-muscled buttocks, those twin engines of pleasure—

She had to stop thinking about twin engines of pleasure, or she would lose it right now.

'What?' Raffa said, swinging round to stare her in the eyes.

'Nothing—'

'Liar. I can see what you're thinking in your eyes—' Sweeping her into his arms, he kissed her. 'And I'm right, aren't I?'

'This won't change my mind,' she insisted as he dropped kisses on her mouth. 'I'm going back to Skavanga just as soon as we've finished our business here.'

He laughed. 'I'm not even going to ask what type of business you're referring to.' Lowering her onto the bed, he hummed with appreciation as he kissed his way down her body. 'You do taste different.'

'Better?'

'Different,' he argued, stretching out his length against her. 'Rich and full—'

'Like a carton of cream?'

'Like pregnant—'

Making love with Raffa was different this time. He didn't tease her as he usually did, and there was a new intensity in the way he looked at her, the way he touched her, and it was a dangerous development in their relationship that made her want to stay with him for ever and not just for the birth.

He was totally devoted to Leila as he made love to her. They had never been so relaxed with each other, or so intimate. He'd never felt so close. Yes, they'd had sex many times, but nothing like this. This was reassurance from him to her, his pledge to Leila that whatever happened in the future the child they'd made would always be a bond between them. He took her slowly and with infinite care, but these slow, careful thrusts were as potent as their wildest sex had ever been, and she lost control almost immediately, her fingers biting into him as she screamed his name until he soothed her down.

'Remind me to teach you some control,' he teased her when she quietened.

'Must you?' she teased back.

'Do you think I'm going to let you glut yourself every time?'

'Why not?' She smiled, and there was mischief in her eyes. Then, lacing her fingers through his hair, she brought him close again for more.

How could he resist this woman? Thrusting deep, he took her over the edge again, and again. He never tired of watching Leila lose control in his arms. It was the best; it was a sign she felt safe with him. And he would keep her safe. He would keep the baby safe too. However accommodating Leila might think him, nothing had changed. She would give birth to their child at a place of his choosing, which meant here on the island. He would not risk Leila's life.

Abuelita was right when she said they were well matched for stubbornness, but where the birth of a child and the life of a mother were concerned he would take no chances, so, whatever Leila thought, in this instance history proved he did know best.

He cemented the growing closeness between them with a visit to his inner sanctum. Leila had already toured the cutting and sorting rooms in his laboratories on the island, as well as the design studio, but now he wanted to show her some of the world's greatest treasures. As well as being a businessman, he was an avid collector of gems with an interesting history. These remarkable items had only been seen by his grandmother, along with a handful of sheikhs, sultans and assorted potentates, who appreciated the chance to view collections similar to their own.

Lights flashed on automatically as they entered the vault. The walls and floor were black marble, while the display cases were formed from blast-proof glass. He wasn't surprised to hear Leila gasp. The lighting had been specifically designed to startle the visitor with a blaze of refracted light from the jewels from the moment they entered the chamber.

'I thought that first vault you showed me was incredible, but this is something else,' she murmured as he led her forward.

He started the tour by explaining the difference between a diadem and a tiara. 'The tiara is more of a semicircular headband, while the diadem is like a crown.' And when Leila expressed her preference for an elaborate diadem set with removable emerald pendants, he suggested she try it on.

'Will you help me?'

'It would be my pleasure.'

'Mine too, I'm sure.' She laughed as he pushed

back her hair and settled the priceless masterpiece on her head.

And somehow her clothes found their way to the floor and the sight of Leila, naked, seated on one of the display tables, wearing only a diamond crown, was a sight he knew would be branded on his mind for ever. It certainly added a frisson to their lovemaking, as she had to sit very straight and still, so the crown didn't fall off her head.

'What happens when I—?'

'No extravagant movements,' he warned.

'I'm not sure about that,' she wailed.

'You have to keep still, Leila, or I'll have to stop—'

'Don't you dare stop!' she warned him as he moved steadily back and forth.

Basking in sensation, he watched her closely, listening to her breathing quicken so he knew exactly when to hold her still.

'Thank goodness you caught the crown,' she panted out a good time later.

'No problem,' he said, settling the priceless diadem back on its stand.

'This is your playroom, isn't it?' she challenged him as she slipped down from the table and moved to inspect the next display case in line.

'But you're the first playmate I've brought in here. And the last,' he assured her when she shot him a mock-warning look.

'I'm pleased to hear it,' she murmured as she leaned over the glass. 'What do we have in here?'

'Some of the world's most valuable coloured diamonds,' he said, more interested in stroking the lush curve of her buttocks as he moved behind her.

'They're amazing—' She gasped as he moved in close and his hands found her breasts.

'Pale blue diamonds like your eyes,' he murmured, weighing her breasts appreciatively. 'And bright pink diamonds like your nipples—'

'Just don't suggest canary yellow like my teeth,' she warned him, starting to laugh.

'I don't generally deal in pearls, except that link I showed you, but if I did, your teeth would certainly compare.'

'Cheese—'

He silenced her in the most obvious way. 'Lean over a little more,' he coaxed. 'Take a closer look inside the case.'

'A much closer look,' Leila agreed, gasping with pleasure as he settled deep.

'Hold on,' he warned. 'The display case is bolted to the floor, so it can take some hammering,' he added re-assuringly.

She laughed, but was eager to do everything he asked to increase her pleasure.

'The diamonds light up the room,' he murmured, continuing to move steadily. 'Would you like me to tell you where some of the most famous pink diamonds in the world are found?'

'Are you kidding me? I couldn't concentrate if you offered me a dozen on a plate.' Standing on tiptoe, she gasped for breath as she thrust her buttocks towards him, giving him better access.

'East Kimberley in Western Australia—Leila, I really don't think your mind's fully on this tutorial—'

'Oh, it is,' she assured him, arching her back so he could see what he was doing.

Forget the diamonds. Taking firm hold of her buttocks, he enjoyed her, and, from the sounds she was making as he moved fast and hard, Leila was enjoying him too.

'So? What did you think of the visit?' he asked when they finally left the facility.

'Thrilling,' she admitted dryly.

Linking his fingers through hers as they strolled to the car, he pulled her close. 'One day the Skavanga mine will produce diamonds as fine as those I just showed you.'

'Then I'd better make sure the display cabinets in the museum are securely bolted to the floor.'

His gaze warmed with amusement. 'It would be a wise precaution,' he agreed.

'Can we display some of those treasures you just showed me in the museum?'

Raffa narrowed his eyes. 'We are still talking about the diamonds, bad girl?'

'Of course we are. I'm not sharing you with anyone.'

He was as sure as he could be that he had overcome all Leila's arguments when it came to the birth of the baby. The way she was resting her head on his shoulder, the way her arm was locked around his waist. He'd never felt closer to anyone, and Leila was giving every signal that she felt this way too. It wasn't a triumph, it was an enormous relief for him, and when they reached the car, he pressed her back against it and whispered in her ear, 'I want you again.'

'What shall we do about it?' she said, pretending surprise.

'Get home fast?' he suggested.

'Why not here?' she challenged, glancing around.

'Because everyone will be pouring out of work soon, and I don't want to frighten them.'

'Here in the shadows quickly?' She was looking over her shoulder at a handy covey of trees.

'Better still, in the car quickly. I love an element of danger, don't you?'

'Yes, I do,' Leila agreed with her mouth very close to his lips. 'It's far more exciting.'

'And you're the quiet sister?'

'That's what they call me.'

'Then they are mistaken.'

'Thank goodness for that,' she said, shooting him a wicked look as she climbed into the car.

He followed and knelt in the footwell, pulling Leila forward to the very edge of the seat.

The next week was highly charged at night, and hectic by day. They shared bed, bath and every available surface in his apartment at the castle, while in their working hours he took Leila through each department in turn so she could understand the process of turning polished gems into priceless works of art. She was an able student on both sides of the divide, and inevitably they grew even closer, sharing humour, facts and preferences, and learning more about each other every day. He was confident she'd stay on. Why would she leave the island when she had everything she could possibly need right here?

He was feeling upbeat when he went to collect Leila for supper, and when he knocked on the door of her turret room, she called, 'Come in...'

'What the hell?' There had been nothing in her voice to give him the slightest clue that he would find her packing a suitcase.

'Your grandmother rang to say she was taking the jet to London tomorrow,' Leila explained cheerfully, shaking out a dress. 'She asked if I'd like to hitch a lift with her.'

'She did what?' he interrupted softly.

'She didn't tell you?'

'What do you think, Leila?' Impulsive trips were right up his grandmother's street, but why had she asked Leila along? And why the hell had Leila accepted her invitation. Why was Leila leaving?

'Why didn't you tell me? When were you going to tell me, Leila? When you got back to Skavanga?'

'Don't be angry with me, Raffa. We both knew I couldn't stay here for ever.'

'That's news to me.'

'No,' she said firmly. 'I always said I'd be going back to Skavanga to have the baby. I never misled you. I told you several times.'

She had, but he had thought she would come round—that she had come round.

'I need to get back before I'm too far down the road with this pregnancy, so I can start planning the exhibition.'

'The exhibition?' he echoed with disbelief. 'Can't you leave that to someone else?'

'No. You know how I feel about the museum and I thought you would be keen for me to get on with the work as we'd planned.'

'Without telling me first that you were going?'

'I knew you were busy today, so I was going to tell you tonight.'

'In bed or out of it?'

'That's not fair, Raffa. I was going to tell you as soon as I saw you. It was a last-minute thing—I had no idea your grandmother was going to London, and the connections to Skavanga are excellent from there.'

He was beyond fury, beyond words. He shook his head as he struggled for control. 'You could at least have done me the courtesy of speaking to me before leaving the island with our unborn child. But then I suppose you've got everything you want out of me now, so it's time for you to go—'

'No!' Leila's face was a mask of outrage as she interrupted him. 'That's never been the type of relationship we have. Please be reasonable, Raffa.'

'Reasonable?' What place did reason have to play where the birth of his child was concerned? 'You're not going anywhere, Leila.'

'Don't be ridiculous!' she said as he moved to bar the door. 'You can't stop me leaving. Short of locking me in and making sure I miss that flight, I'm going home tomorrow. It's time for me to leave. You won't share your hang-ups with me, so we've gone as far as we can. I told you everything, Raffa.' Looking disappointed in him, she shook her head. 'And you've told me precisely nothing. You want to control everything without giving me any reason for why you must do so—and if I can't understand you, what chance have we got? I wouldn't just walk out without saying anything. I was going to thank you before I left—'

'You were going to thank me?' he echoed, leaning back against the ancient door. 'Am I supposed to be grateful for that?'

But everything Leila said was right. He couldn't open up to anyone, not even Leila, but he had been utterly convinced that she would stay.

'Raffa, please,' she said, closing the lid of her suitcase. 'It's all arranged. My onward ticket's booked. It's not as if I'm disappearing as you and my brother so often do. You know where I am. You can come visit any time you want.'

Leila was dictating terms now? '*Dios,* Leila! You're having my baby. You can't just walk out like this.'

'Were you planning to hold me prisoner on the island until I gave birth?'

The silence hung between them and then she laughed without humour. 'You were,' she whispered incredulously.

'I only want to keep you safe.'

'There you go again—I don't understand why this obsession with keeping me safe when I'm just as safe in Skavanga. You can't micromanage the birth, as if it were a business, Raffa.'

Leila couldn't know the depth of his fears for her, and as he couldn't tell her they had reached stalemate.

'I'm leaving the country, Raffa,' she stated firmly. 'But I'll only be a plane ride away, so please don't be angry with me.'

'Am I to suppose my grandmother called you up out of the blue?'

'Well, yes, she did, actually.'

He had to confess, it would hardly be the first time his grandmother had acted impetuously. She was probably visiting her own doctor in London when she thought of Leila, and had wanted some company on the flight.

There was a wistful look in Leila's eyes that told him she wished things could be different, almost as if she wished he would beg her to stay. He had been so fixated on the birth, he hadn't given much thought to the future. He supposed now he had imagined Leila getting on with her life as he got on with his after the birth of their child. They would live separate lives, and only meet up when they handed their child over for a visit—

Dios! Just the thought of that made him sick. The idea of handing a child back and forth, like a parcel—

Leila's eyes were full of tears as if she was waiting for him to say something that would make things right between them, but his life had been built on objectivity, not emotion, and he didn't have any answers she'd want to hear.

'You always knew we had to get on with our lives at some point, Raffa. I haven't even had my first scan yet.'

'Well, you can have that here.'

'I've already booked one in Skavanga. I could send you a photograph.'

Shaking his head, he said a flat, 'No.' Why bother? What use was a photograph to him?

Leila deserved stability, security and a storybook ending with a man who could feel emotion. He couldn't offer her that. As always when emotions threatened, ice had already closed around his heart. And even if he let her go, he could still control every aspect of the birth, but from a distance.

'*Bon voyage,* Leila,' he said coolly. 'As you so rightly say, you'll only be a short plane ride away.'

CHAPTER ELEVEN

SHE HELD OUT until Raffa left the room and then she crumpled. So much for self-determination. Someone should have warned her how much it sucked. Did Britt feel like this after one of her storming tirades? Did Eva fold like a wilting leaf with ice flowing through her veins instead of blood? When her sisters acted steely, was it all a sham?

The temptation to return to being the quiet little mouse was overwhelming. She might have done, had it not been for the child growing inside her, the child who depended on her to get things right. There was never going to be a good time to leave Raffa. And she'd learned a lot while she'd been here. She'd changed, discovered her own seam of strength. Maybe it had always been there, but quietly.

Raffa, with all his talk of the 'top men for the job', wanting to control every element of the birth, had put everything in perspective for her. She had grown to love him, and now she couldn't love him more, but she had no expectation of him loving her back. She doubted Raffa even had the capacity to love. His reaction when she had offered to send him a photograph of the scan had been proof enough of that.

It was that thought that broke her, and, like a wounded

animal, she buried her head in her arms and bayed her frustration into the empty, uncaring room. But even that was an indulgence. She had to be strong for the baby, and so standing up she faced the brutal truth. Would an aristocrat like Don Rafael Leon seriously consider progressing a relationship with Leila Skavanga, a small-town girl who worked in a mine beyond the Arctic Circle, whose father had been a drunk and whose mother had been his punchbag?

The thought of her mother made her cry again. Be bold in all you do. Was she being bold, or was she being stubborn?

It wasn't always easy to be strong, Leila concluded, even with a baby to consider. There were times when she missed her mother with a huge aching pain, and this was one of those times, but she wasn't going to throw her mother's wishes to the four winds. She was going to take them and make them count for something. She would turn the Skavanga Diamond exhibition into a talking point around the world. And she would write Raffa a note before she left, setting him free, and at the same time promising not to cut him out of their baby's life. It had taken two to make this precious child, but she would bring it up, and she would give birth in Skavanga, without fuss or the 'best man for the job' standing over her.

At last the call connected. By which time he was almost jumping out of his skin with frustration. 'Grandmother. What the hell are you doing?'

'Why, Rafael,' his grandmother tempered, slowing down his heated oratory at a stroke. 'This must be a serious call for you to give me my Sunday title.'

'You know it's serious. How could you do this to me?'

'How could *I* do this to you, Rafael?' There was a pause. 'Maybe I'm saving you from yourself by taking Leila with me.'

He gave a short dismissive laugh. 'Destroying me would be closer to the truth. Don't you know how much it means to me to keep her here so I can supervise the birth?'

'Don't you know how much I love you, Rafael?'

He let the silence hang. 'You know I do,' he growled at last.

'Then trust me, Rafael. I do know what I'm doing.'

'I hope so.' It was a fight to keep the anger from his voice, but he had always respected his grandmother too much to lose control when he was speaking to her.

'I know you think you should be doing something more, Rafael, but you can't control everything.'

'I can try.'

'You certainly can't force Leila to obey you. She has a mind of her own, that one.'

'There's no need to sound quite so pleased about it.'

'If you trap a wild bird, Rafael, it will die.'

'And if you set it free?'

'Time will prove me right or wrong,' his grandmother insisted calmly. 'Well? Aren't you going to wish me *bon voyage,* grandson?'

Gritting his teeth he managed, 'Safe journey, and a speedy return home, Abuelita.'

Being on the private jet with Raffa's grandmother was informal and fun—or it could have been if the aircraft hadn't been taking Leila away from the man she loved.

'There's no shame in a little fear when the plane takes off,' Raffa's grandmother said briskly, handing over a wad of tissues.

Leila had no fear of flying. Her only fear was losing Raffa, who had brushed her off so easily.

'Better now?' the dowager enquired once they were airborne.

Tipping her head with a wry smile, Leila nodded. 'Much better, thank you.'

'We're survivors, you and I, Leila. Nothing gets us down for long. We're like corks that bob up again, and we learn from setbacks, don't we?'

Leila nodded wryly. 'Promise you'll come and see me in Skavanga when the baby's born.'

'Try and keep me away. But I'm going to ask something of you in return.'

'To visit you?' Leila guessed.

'Correct.' The old lady's gaze was unwavering as she offered Leila her hand to seal the pact.

'Deal,' Leila agreed softly.

'And now I'm going to tell you some things about Rafael that he would never tell you himself. I didn't tell you before because I've always kept my grandson's confidence, but I can't sit back and watch Rafael destroy the best thing that's ever happened to him—that's you and your baby, in case you're in any doubt, Leila.'

Deep down, Leila supposed she had always known that this particular old lady never did anything by chance, and the flight to London was the perfect opportunity for them to have a one-to-one.

'Rafael reminds me of his grandfather so much. Although—' The dowager made a whimsical gesture with her hands. 'Rafael has his reasons for being the way he is, while my husband had no excuse.'

'But you loved him?'

'I adored him,' Raffa's grandmother corrected her. 'Who wants a weak man? Not me. You were crying because of Rafael when we took off, and not some fear of flying.'

'I was very sad to leave the island,' Leila confessed guardedly.

'And that's not all,' the dowager said briskly. 'I don't think you're frightened of anything except your own heart, Leila Skavanga. You're certainly not frightened of flying, though you've got every reason to be after your parents' accident.'

'Strangely it's never affected me that way.'

'Because the crash was no accident?' the dowager suggested when Leila hesitated. 'The press suggested your father was drunk at the controls.'

The dowager's frankness was refreshing and it tempted Leila to unburden thoughts that had plagued her for years. 'Or maybe my mother seized control because she'd had enough.'

'And sent them both plummeting to their deaths.'

'Being controlled isn't pretty,' Leila agreed.

'But you would never allow yourself to be controlled by anyone. And if I tell you that Rafael's mother died giving birth to him, then perhaps you can understand his fears for you a little better.'

Oh, no. Oh, no. Oh, no.

'I had no idea.'

'And Rafael wouldn't want you to know. He wouldn't want to frighten you, so he would never tell you, which is why I wanted this opportunity to have you to myself. Your safety is driving him crazy, Leila. That's why Rafael feels he must control every aspect of this baby's birth.'

He found the note right away. Leila had left it on his pillow. He ground his jaw and seriously considered tearing it up. What could it tell him that he didn't already know? Leaning back against the wall, he opened the envelope. There was one sheet of paper inside. The short note might as well have begun 'Dear John'.

It was a polite, emotion-free deed of separation. It was a reasonable and considered application to remain friends. It was an offer of complete access to his child at any time of his choosing—providing that access took place in Skavanga. Leila didn't want anything from him—no child support, no help with housing, no money, nothing. Though she promised to keep him in the loop— so kind of her. Thanks to him and his excellent introduction to the diamond industry, she intended to pursue her studies and take a Masters degree in Gemology—in Skavanga, of course. It was at that point he ripped the note to shreds and tossed it in the bin. Leila had rocked his world with her abrupt departure. If it hadn't been for the baby—

He would never see her again?

But there was a baby, and that baby had to be born and he had to know Leila would come through that birth safely. It wasn't enough for him to write the cheques and pull the strings. He had to *know.* This was as much a part of his nature as stubbornness was part of Leila's character. He had to see for himself that she survived the birth, for as much as he resented the way Leila had cut herself free he would happily die rather than harm her in any way.

The dowager had fallen asleep, leaving Leila to mull over her incredible revelation. Knowing Raffa's mother had died in childbirth explained so much about him. Now she knew why he wanted to control the birth of their child. It wasn't to exert his authority over her, as she had supposed, but simply to keep her safe.

And what had she done?

She had cut all ties with him, leaving no loose ends. There was no way back. She had always believed a clean break was for the best, having been used to radical change in her life from a very young age. But had she tried to get to know him—really tried? She felt like curling into a cringing ball at the thought of how selfish she'd been.

'Have you, dear?'

Leila blinked, realising she must have spoken out loud. 'I'm afraid I've only been thinking about myself.'

'I've been saying the same thing to Rafael for years,' his grandmother remarked. 'If you ask me, it's time both of you took your blinkers off.'

It seemed so long since she had left the island, and her personal world had been spinning in the wrong direction ever since. Wrong, because it never brought her any closer to Raffa. As far as her work was concerned, it couldn't have been better. Preparing the site for the exhibition was going well, but there hadn't been a word from Raffa, who had thrown all his considerable resources behind Leila to make sure she had all the help she could possibly need for her work from his team. And why should there be any word from Raffa, when she had made it quite clear in her letter to him that it was over between them for good?

But now she'd had her scan she had to talk to him as a matter of urgency. She'd had some really big news. She'd tried all the various numbers she had been given for him, including his PA, who was cagey about Raffa's whereabouts, and even his grandmother. Sharif and

Roman might have been able to tell her, but she didn't want to get into the inevitable conversation with them, and so she called Britt.

'Who knows?' Britt said, yawning as if she had just woken up. 'We haven't heard from him.'

Leila could hear Sharif murmuring in the background and realised they must be in bed together. She couldn't get off the phone fast enough. She thought about ringing Eva, but didn't want to be subjected to the third degree.

What did Leila know about Raffa Leon? She didn't even know where he was, or how to contact him. How she longed to be in his arms now, confiding in him, but she'd made too good a job of driving him away.

'The babies are doing fine, thank you,' she informed the empty air. 'Our twins are doing fine, Raffa.'

To hell with control! To hell with all Leila's protestations that she was fine and could live without him, and her sisters' insistence that Leila needed space. He'd given her long enough and the birth of their child was imminent. He'd kept a watching brief on her from a distance. She attended check-ups regularly. She ate sensibly, worked reasonable hours and got plenty of rest. She was the model of a modern working mother-to-be. He should be satisfied with that, but he wasn't about to leave her to go through the birth alone.

'You're clear to go, Romeo-Lima-two-five-eight—'

'Roger, Control.' Opening the throttle on the twin engines, he released the brakes.

For a time he was content to let his spirit soar with the jet. Every second took him closer to Leila and the answers he could only find when they were together. She'd got under his skin. Leila Skavanga had invaded every part of him. Life was vivid Technicolor with her.

Without her it was a dull, stormy grey. Levelling off, he handed over the controls to his co-pilot.

'Coffee, Tyr?'

'No milk,' the powerfully built Viking reminded him.

Removing his headphones, he left the cockpit. Both he and Leila had secrets. His was possibly the hardest to keep. Leila's brother was back in her life. She just didn't know it yet, but it wasn't up to him to break the news. Tyr would let his sisters know he was back when he was ready.

The flight attendants jumped to attention as Raffa walked into the galley.

'I'll sort myself out,' he told them as politely as he could and they quickly made themselves scarce. It was a rare beast that challenged him when he was in this mood. Leila would challenge him, but Leila wasn't frightened of anyone.

He went through the mechanics of assembling two strong cups of coffee. Why the hell did he miss her so much? It wasn't as if Leila was easy. She was quiet but she challenged him constantly, and was possibly the strongest woman he had ever known.

And now it was coming up to Christmas and she shouldn't be on her own. Her sisters and their husbands were away for the holidays, and he couldn't bear to think of Leila alone.

With a shrug and a smile he reached for the satellite phone.

CHAPTER TWELVE

SHE WAS STILL working and intended to carry on until the museum closed its doors on Christmas Eve. She'd be back in the new year if she hadn't given birth by then.

She was all organised. The cards were written, the presents were wrapped, the fire was lit and the house was glowing. Christmas was going to be great. She was going to decorate the nursery over the holidays, and finish the baby shawl she had painstakingly knitted, unpicked and knitted again, until she got it—well, almost right. She had baked too, taking round little pies and cakes as gifts to her neighbours, so the house smelled great. The baby stuff was piled in a corner waiting to be set out in the nursery—the best part—the reward for all her labours. She only had a short time to go now. The doctor had said she might deliver early, as it was twins.

There was only one thing missing from her Christmas preparations, Leila reflected as she sat on the rug, hugging her knees in front of the fire, and that was this man... Picking up the newspaper, she stared at the ridiculously handsome face before reading the banner headline. Bite-sized pieces of the text jumped out at her: *Don Rafael Leon... Famous Spanish billionaire... Strikes gold again... Battles a sandstorm in Kareshi... Risking his life—*

Her heart stopped. Clenching the newspaper, she wished Raffa would stop risking his life. Why did he have to do that? Why couldn't he slow down for once? *Why couldn't he be here?*

Why hadn't she heard from him? Rubbing her face on her hands, she thought back to how determined she'd been to handle this birth alone, and how reluctantly Raffa had granted her wish. Now she understood why he was so concerned and why he had his people watching out for her—her own doctor had told her about the regular calls from Raffa's doctor, taking the opportunity to reassure Leila that professional confidence between doctor and patient extended to everyone, even other doctors. Her doctor had even taken calls from Raffa, though he never left a number, but why would he, when Leila had told him in that letter not to get in touch?

That wretched letter! Why had she left it for him in the first place? To be fair? To be fair to Raffa? Sanctimonious twaddle! What was that about? What had she been thinking? Hormones had been thinking for her, obviously. Why couldn't he be here? Where was he? Was he even safe? Why did two of the best men in her life have to disappear? Was she jinxed?

She wanted to tell him she understood everything now. She wanted to hold him and be strong for him. Pressing her head into her knees, she fought back tears, knowing she had to be strong for their babies. Lifting her chin, she straightened out the newspaper and read on: *Raffa Leon, bringing back more fabulous gems to be set with the now famous Skavanga Diamonds.*

Raffa and his colleagues in the consortium had made Skavanga a household name. When she'd been on the island with him and had asked the secret of his success, he'd said good product and publicity, along with a unique selling point, adding that, yes, there were fabulous gems on show in his underground vaults, but his most valuable stock was kept in an underground cave guarded by gryphons and dragons...

The tears were back when she remembered how they'd laughed. They'd been in bed at the time—

No. Bed. Thoughts.

Not now. Not ever. Finished. Done with. Bed thoughts—specifically sex thoughts of any kind, especially those involving intimate moments between them—were absolutely forbidden. Raffa's humour and his tender asides—those were forbidden too. She had to stop thinking about him, or she'd never ease this ache inside her.

So, what was he doing for Christmas?

Leila stared round her cosy home. Would he be somewhere nice like this, or in some sterile hotel? With the glow of the fire, and the red ribbons and candles she had brought down from the box in the eaves, it looked so warm and welcoming. There was just one thing missing...

Oh, if this wasn't the biggest pity party of all time. She'd be dressing up in a red robe, sticking cotton wool to her cheeks and giving herself gifts out of a trash sack in a minute. She was well organised, with plenty of food. She was safe and warm. What more did she want?

Don't even think the name.

That lasted all of five seconds.

She'd posted Raffa's card early, along with a special card for his *abuelita.* She had kept Raffa's card carefully neutral. 'Wishing you a wonderful Christmas and the very best New Year ever. Leila x'

That wasn't thinking his name. That was running a mental checklist to make sure she hadn't left anyone off her list. She'd sent Raffa the type of card she would send to a close friend—a friend close enough not to need an update on her status, because he already knew enough about her life, and yet distant enough to suggest she was back in harness in her old life, and quite happily getting on with it.

Except for the yawning great crater in her chest where her heart used to be.

She wasn't going to think like that...

Was the house always this quiet?

She looked at her phone and then remembered she'd turned it off. Her sisters were driving her mad by email, saying it was too close to the birth of the baby and she should turn her phone on. But she didn't want to speak to anyone—unless that someone was Raffa. And as he wasn't about to call...

Glancing out of the window at the fat flakes of snow tumbling down, she smiled wistfully at the thought of Raffa becoming a local hero. He'd certainly helped to put Skavanga on the map again. The Skavanga Diamond brand was already famous across the world, and the people of Skavanga loved him for it.

The town had been failing for so long, with Britt battling tirelessly to keep everything afloat, and then the consortium came along, and now it was like Christmas every day. They'd all worked hard to make Skavanga a success. There was a café at the museum now, as well as a playground for the children, and film installations showing diamonds in production from rocks to sparkling gems...

Ho hum...

The fire crackled, the snow pattered lightly against the window. Now what should she do?

Oh, come on! She'd eaten supper. It was almost bed-time. Wasn't this the time she looked forward to the most? Not just for sleep and oblivion, and a chance to dream, but to get out her small hoard of baby stuff…to touch it, to fold it, to hold it to her face…

She could spend some time thinking about the twins before she went to bed. What could be better than that?

The twins Raffa didn't know about yet.

Hugging her enormous belly, Leila bit her lip anxiously. Why couldn't anyone tell her where Raffa was? He had to be the most elusive man on the planet. Should she leave him to enjoy the festivities in peace? Or should she keep trying those numbers Britt had told her to try? She didn't want to bother her sisters again so close to Christmas. She looked at her phone. Small. Silent. Off. Described it to a tee.

But there was nothing to stop her trying those numbers one more time. If Raffa was busy at least he'd know she'd been trying to get hold of him. Picking the phone up, she stared at it for a few tense seconds, and then, closing her eyes, she held down the button to turn it on—

And jumped when it rang immediately.

'Leila? Is that you?'

Raffa!

'Where the hell have you been, Leila?'

'Ha…aa…'

'Is that any type of answer?'

Paralysed with surprise, she could hardly speak. Hearing Raffa's voice had shocked her rigid. Hugging the phone so close to her face it must have left an imprint in her skin, she drank in the sound of his voice. He could have said anything— He could have ordered pizza and she would still have tears running down her face. Just to hear him… Just to know he was safe.

She had to pull the phone away from her ear for a moment to draw a deep, shuddering breath and compose herself, before she could manage a steady, 'Hello, Raffa... What a surprise...'

'If you say it's nice to hear from me, I'll find you and spank you, pregnant or not. Why have you had your phone turned off?'

'Erm...I couldn't sleep. So I turned it off and forgot to turn it on again.'

'I saw all your calls listed and was worried to death. I've been trying to call you non-stop.'

'Sorry...' She caressed the phone. He'd been trying to call her. Lovely phone. She'd never turn it off again. Ever.

'I spoke to your sisters, and all they'd say was you'd gone to ground, and that maybe you needed some space. The way they said it made it sound like space from me, so...'

'So you were speaking to Eva, I'm guessing,' Leila supplied as her head began to clear.

'Maybe,' Raffa agreed wryly.

He didn't want to get her sister into trouble. That was nice.

'And did you? Do you?' he pressed urgently. 'Need space, I mean. Talk to me, Leila. I need to hear your voice.'

Raffa needed to hear her voice. She looked around the room as if the furniture would be good enough to confirm that she was actually awake and this wasn't one of her nightly Raffa dreams. 'I'm fine now. I don't need space now,' she added in case he thought he should ring off. Better release her death grip on the phone before her fingers dropped off. She couldn't hold him on the line by strangling the receiver.

'So you're well, Leila?'

She was now with Raffa's voice rolling over her like honey. 'Quite well, thank you.'

'Quite well.' He laughed at the prim expression. 'Your doctor wouldn't tell me anything—apart from the fact that I shouldn't worry as you were in good health and the pregnancy was progressing as planned.'

'Doctor-patient confidentiality,' she agreed, silently thanking her lucky stars that Raffa hadn't heard the news about their twins yet. She couldn't bear him to hear that from anyone else. And she wasn't about to tell him over the phone. 'So, where are you now?'

'Outside your door.'

What?

'Did you hear me, Leila?'

'You're as bad as my brother.' She flared as her heart went crazy. When Tyr disappeared they never knew when he was coming back. 'Sorry…' She composed herself—just about. 'I heard you.'

'Well? Aren't you going to let me in?'

Like a runner off the blocks she catapulted into action, or rather she used her unusual weight distribution as leverage to stumble forward and up, slowly straightening until she was upright. Turning full circle, which was harder than it sounded when your belly took up half the room, she hardly knew where to begin. Heading for the door by a circuitous route so she could plump cushions and straighten throws as she went, she couldn't help wonder how a wood shack would stand up to a castle.

Cosy. It was cosy. And she loved it and lived in every inch of it, that was how.

The door was the only thing between them now. She could sense Raffa standing behind it as she stretched out her hand and wrapped it around the handle. Taking one steadying breath, she flung the door wide.

He looked amazing.

Never mind that. Forget the impulse to fling herself into his arms with relief. Raffa had been out of contact for months. The right thing to do was to stand back and be cool with him—

To hell with that!

Flinging her arms around his neck, she hugged him as if her life depended on it. 'Raffa!' The air was cold and frosty, and his stubble-roughened cheek was cold, but he smelled warm and delicious, and he was every bit as solid and fabulous as she remembered. 'How wonderful to see you.'

'You too, Leila,' he said quietly.

Untangling herself, she stood back, feeling rather stupid. That was a ridiculous greeting to give someone she hadn't seen for months, and now she couldn't gauge Raffa's reaction to her overly excited puppy act. He was taking his time to look her up and down as her cheeks fired with embarrassment. 'Won't you come in? Please, come in out of the cold...' And give me chance to compose myself, she thought as she turned her back on him.

Closing the door once Raffa was inside, she turned around. Muffled up in a heavy dark jacket and jeans, he looked insanely handsome. And she loved him so much that was crazy too, especially as her love had no basis in hope or reality. She couldn't help herself. She was nuts about him. And would have to hide it, if this wasn't going to be the most embarrassing encounter of all time.

'Nice,' he said, glancing round the cabin.

There was genuine warmth in his voice and she relaxed a little, enough to tell him, 'The cabin has been in our family for generations.'

'You're very lucky, Leila—to have such a history. And such a strong bond with a place.'

Unlike Raffa, she thought, remembering what his grandmother had told her about his youth. 'Yes, I am,' she agreed as he continued to look around.

What a lot of space he took up, and the little that was left was filled with his energy. She'd never think of the cabin the same way again, she realised as Raffa absent-mindedly shrugged off his jacket in response to the cosy heat. She took it from him. It was still warm from his body and she tucked her hands inside it as she went to hang it up.

'When you said you lived in a cabin, I had no idea what to expect,' he admitted, 'but you've made such a lovely home here. And the surroundings… The lake, the trees, the mountains, the drive here—it's all spectacular.' The sexy mouth pressed down as he shrugged. 'No wonder you never want to leave Skavanga.'

Never leaving Skavanga suddenly seemed an unreasonable penalty for leaving the rest of the world and Raffa Leon behind. 'Skavanga's lovely, but it's nice to get away from here too.'

'To the island?'

'Your island is beautiful, Raffa.'

'Yes, it is.'

His gaze lingered, warming her face. It was as if they were both reading each other, searching for clues, looking for changes. Just hearing Raffa's voice in her home was like having the most beautiful soundtrack to a romantic film playing. It wasn't so much the words he used, but the timbre, the pitch—

And was this a good idea? she wondered as they continued to stare at each other. There was so much to catch up on, so much to work through.

'Sit, Leila. You look tired.'

She sank into a chair with relief, while Raffa went to examine some of the old sepia prints on the wall. Just seeing him had exhausted her. Emotional overload, she reasoned, combined with pregnancy hormones on red alert.

'We used to come here for holidays with our grandparents,' she explained as he moved down the row of photographs, scrutinising each one in turn. 'This was the first prospectors' hut, but we've improved the cabin over the years—'

She stopped as Raffa flashed an amused glance at her. 'So you have inside facilities now?'

'Can you seriously imagine Britt using a bucket?'

They both laughed and the tension eased a little. Maybe this visit would turn out okay after all.

'As the mine took off a lot of other people started to build cabins in the vicinity,' she explained as Raffa peered out of the window.

'Sorry—I'm expecting a van to turn up, and I don't want to keep the men waiting outside in the cold.'

'A van?'

'With supplies.'

'Oh…'

Her brain refused to compute this, but she must have frowned, because Raffa shrugged. 'If you don't want them, send them back. But there's food too, so let's have supper first.'

She smiled. 'You're hungry.'

'No time to eat,' he confirmed. 'Long flight, long drive, but worth it.'

As Raffa fell silent she realised he was trying to see the newspaper she'd been so avidly reading with his photograph prominently displayed. She should have closed it up before she opened the door and heeled it under the seat now. 'Would you like to sit down?'

'Why? Do I make the place look untidy?' he suggested, turning to shoot a wry smile at her.

No. You make it seem small.

Pulling back from the window, Raffa turned to face her, and, leaning back against the wall with his arms folded across his chest, he smiled, the flash of strong white teeth showing in stark contrast to his burnished skin. 'It's good to see you again, Leila.'

'You've been in the desert—'

Raffa waved an admonishing finger at her. 'I told you no questions.'

'Not where Tyr's concerned,' Leila agreed. 'So have you two been working together?'

'Tyr will tell you when he's ready to tell you. So this is the original prospector?' he said, changing the subject as he turned to examine one of the framed photographs on the wall. 'This one here?'

Like Tyr, Raffa was expert at keeping a confidence, Leila realised. She'd get no more out of him. 'That's right. That's my ancestor, the first Skavanga.'

'You don't look a bit like him.'

'I decided in the end that a beard doesn't suit me.'

His cheek creased in a smile. 'You should have this shot hanging in the museum.'

'I'm ahead of you, Señor Leon. A copy's already hanging in the entrance hall.'

'I might have known it, Ms Efficiency.'

She blushed as Raffa's gaze swept her belly. 'How many months are you now, Leila?'

'A month or so to go.' This conversation was so back to front. Her brain was sluggish thanks to pregnancy hormones and still she hadn't got round to telling him about the twins.

'I thought you had longer than that. By my calculations—'

'Your calculations are off.'

'Oh?'

'There are things you couldn't possibly know about, Raffa.'

'Such as?'

Even with that suspicious look on his face Raffa made her heart turn over. Taking a deep breath, she told him, 'Such as, I'm having twins.'

'Twins?' Raffa's voice dropped an octave, and for once he seemed at a loss. Dipping his head, he said, 'Two babies?'

'That is the usual count,' she confirmed, trying to appear light-hearted as she waited for his reaction. Double the expected tally could hardly light up the heart of a man who didn't want children.

Raffa's face lit, then darkened dramatically. He might have frightened her if she hadn't known why. His surprise at what she'd told him had been replaced in an instant by dread at the thought of her giving birth to two babies.

'Your grandmother explained why you feel the way you do,' she said quickly. 'Please don't be angry with her, Raffa,' she added as he glanced at her. 'She only did it because she loves you, and because she knows I love you too.'

There. She'd said it. Her feelings were laid bare before him for him to stamp on if he chose to, but this was too important for her to hold anything back.

Raffa's face revealed nothing. Why should it when he had been hiding his feelings all his life, and when she had brought up a past he would rather forget? 'Your grandmother told me that your mother died giving birth to you,' she said carefully, feeling it was better to get everything out in the open now. 'Apart from your feelings when you were old enough to understand what had happened, she also told me that your father and siblings never allowed you to forget what had happened...'

Reaching out when he still remained silent, she let her hand fall back. Raffa wasn't ready for sympathy. He never had been. That was why he held his feelings close and why he repelled others, especially those with a claim on his emotions.

'Twins,' he murmured. His eyes cleared as he looked at her. 'Really?'

'Really.' She couldn't tell what he was thinking, but at least he was thinking, rather than expressing some knee-jerk reaction. She'd give him more time. She'd give him all the time he needed. 'I haven't asked you if you'd like something to eat or drink,' she said, striving for normality.

'Sorry, Leila— Have to go. The van's just arrived. You stay where you are.' Raffa's hand on her shoulder was gentle and insistent. Crossing the small room, he shrugged on his jacket. 'Baby supplies.' He frowned, as if realising he would have to rethink his plans completely. 'I didn't know how you'd be fixed, so, like I said, I brought food too. We can have a picnic.'

'Sounds like fun.' Or it might have been if Raffa hadn't been so distant.

His mind was fixed on other things. He was still getting over the shock, she reasoned. And who could blame him?

'Relax, Leila. There's no agenda here. Just two friends playing catch-up.'

Of course. She sank back. Hopes crushed. She was so emotional at the moment there was no grey, only black and white. Maybe he didn't want two babies. Raffa hadn't exactly enlisted the town band to herald the first. Why couldn't she tap into calm Leila, the girl who was such a thoughtful, sensible mouse? Why was she sitting here with her heart thumping and her thoughts flying in every direction?

She started with alarm when the door opened and Raffa came in carrying a huge carton. 'No, you stay there,' he insisted when she moved to help him. 'I can manage.'

He didn't want any involvement, she reflected as she hauled herself out of her chair. Going to stare out of the window, she watched him directing the men. After so long apart every glimpse was a gift. And though she had categorically stated she didn't want anything from Raffa, and that she didn't need anything, it made her heart soar to think he'd gone shopping for her.

And she should make him feel welcome in return.

Lumbering into action, she fetched dishes from the cupboard, and soup and salad from the fridge, just in time before he blazed back into the house.

'Coffee on?'

'Yes,' she murmured, belatedly accepting in some part of her pregnancy-scrambled brain that she would have to turn the coffee machine on for coffee to happen. And now the sheer size of Raffa dominating her compact living space—his energy, the sheer power blazing off him—

'Here, let me get that for you—' Reaching across, he took charge of coffee production, and when he pulled back he brushed her body so that now her hands were shaking.

'I've got something to show you,' she blurted.

'Oh?'

Raffa was too busy making coffee to pay much attention.

'Yes…' She looked at him hopefully.

'Good.'

Tears pricked her eyes. She had to remind herself that he didn't have a clue what she was talking about, and that the pregnancy was making her overly emotional. But if he could only show some interest—give some reaction—

It might help if you actually showed him what you're talking about?

Okay, she would. And if he was still aloof and distant when she showed him, at least that was proof she was on her own. And wasn't that what she had always wanted? The babies without the man? Remember that?

What a sad idea that seemed now.

'You all right?' he asked with concern as she sucked in a fast breath in lieu of a sob.

'Yes,' she said, more to convince herself than Raffa.

'Good. Then I'll go and help the men get the rest of the stuff out of the van, so they can get off. You can handle the rest of this? Yes?' he pressed.

'Yes,' she said on autopilot.

It wasn't just food Raffa had brought with him—or even one box of supplies. It was a vanload of baby equipment: baby clothes, toys, a stroller, a Moses basket, a cot, a playpen—the last two flat-packed, requiring assembly, so the last items to make it into the house, courtesy of Raffa and two burly men from the store, were a toolkit, a stack of decorating sheets and a workbench.

'Raffa, please… No more. Stop. It's too much. I can't let you do this—'

'Do what?' he said, paying off the men with a generous tip as he turned to stare at her. 'There's everything you could possibly need—'

'That's just it.'

'What is?' he demanded impatiently.

'I don't need anything.'

'Oh, not that again. You clearly do.' Raffa's gaze swept the room. 'In fact, I'll have to get more stuff on order. Come on, Leila,' he insisted when she began to protest. 'How are you going to hoist a couple of cots up the stairs in your condition?'

'I'll get them delivered and pay to have them assembled, if I have to.'

'And the playpen?'

'I don't need one yet. And when I do I'll assemble it with the instruction sheet laid out in front of me.'

Raffa wasn't even listening. And before she knew it they were staring at each other daggers drawn, arguing about who was in control. 'You can't just walk in here and take over, Raffa. This is my house, my pregnancy—'

'And our children. Never mistake me for a man who could be satisfied with making the odd guest appearance on significant days after the birth, Leila. I'm going to be involved from day one, so get used to it. I'm not trying to compete with any preparations you've made. These are our children. Aren't I entitled to be excited too?'

Raffa, excited? You wouldn't know it from his face. As always, he was perfectly under control. 'Yes, of course you are. And if you'll just stop pacing for a moment, there's something I really want to show you.'

CHAPTER THIRTEEN

'WHAT IS IT, LEILA? What are you going to show me?'

'I wanted to send it to you,' she said as she heaved herself up. 'But you're as good at disappearing as Tyr, and I didn't know when you'd get it—if you'd get it. And I couldn't risk it getting lost in a heap of mail on your desk.'

'Like your email.'

'Like my email,' she confirmed dryly.

'So, what is it? What are we talking about?'

Shrugging her shoulders, she smiled. 'Wait and see.'

He glanced at Leila's swollen stomach as she made her way across the room to a bureau and felt his heart clench. 'You'll need a bigger house,' he murmured, thinking out loud as she rooted through some papers. 'I'll have to order twice as much equipment—'

'I don't need anything, Raffa.'

'You'll trip over that pride of yours one day, Leila. You do need things. Let me help you. These babies are my responsibility too.'

She shrugged and appeared to consider this, but then she turned to him and her face was as open as he remembered when they'd first met. 'I panicked when no one would put me in touch with you—' She was holding something behind her back. 'I was worried about you,

Raffa. I don't think you or Tyr has the slightest idea how many people care about you, or how they worry when you go off radar. For God's sake,' she exclaimed, tears welling in her eyes, 'I've already lost a brother. Do you seriously think I could bear to lose you?'

'You haven't lost Tyr, and you haven't lost me, Leila. I could never reach you when I rang, and I tried I don't know how many times.'

She thought about this for a moment. 'Eva must have told Reception not to put you through. It's the type of thing she does when she's trying to protect me and doesn't realise she's only making things worse. But you're right. I should have tried harder— I should have found some way to tell you—'

'No. I'm just as much to blame,' he agreed. 'Now, show me what you've got behind your back.'

She handed him an envelope.

'What's this?' His guts twisted as he remembered the last time he'd read a letter from Leila.

'I started to write to you, then realised that was about as pointless as putting a letter up the chimney for Santa. And if I sent it to the office, I didn't want it lying forgotten on your desk. It's too important for that. Why don't you open it, Raffa? Please…'

Opening the envelope, he pulled out a small black-and-white photograph. He stared at it in silence. It was an image from the latest scan. Twins. Two little people…one blowing bubbles, while the other sucked his or her thumb.

'Our babies, Raffa,' Leila said gently. 'Your children… and mine.'

Wave after wave of emotion crashed over him. Feelings he'd bottled up for years ran riot inside him. Tears sprang to his eyes, and he had never cried. He could never have predicted that seeing his children would affect him like this.

'Raffa…'

He couldn't speak yet. He couldn't think coherently. All he wanted to do was to stare at the image on the tiny piece of paper.

'Please don't disappear again, Raffa. I was so frightened for you.'

Still holding the scan, he turned slowly to look at Leila. He doubted he could ever bear to be parted from this small piece of evidence, let alone give it back to her.

'Raffa?' she said again.

Shaking himself round, he went to kneel at her feet, and, taking her hands in his, he held them tightly. 'Leila… Look at me. I'm so sorry. I should never have left you. I should never have listened to you and your ridiculous notion that you needed space, or to my own stubborn belief that who I am is cast in stone. We're both far too stubborn, you and I.'

A small smile crept onto her face. 'How could I have contacted you if I needed you? Never do that to me again, Raffa. We're not alone any more. We have these two to think about.'

As she spoke Leila stroked her hand over the curve of her belly, and as his grip tightened on the scan he knew his life had changed for ever. And for the better by far.

She laughed softly. 'It would probably be more convenient for everyone if I were still Leila the peacemaker, the sister who goes along with what everyone else wants for the sake of a quiet life—'

'Strange. I've never seen you like that, Leila—'

She huffed with amusement. 'Whether you have or not, I can't be like that ever again, because I'm going to be a mother and I've got these two to think about.'

Her face lit up. 'Two babies at one time! Who'd have thought it?'

'I would. And you've never been the mouse you think you are. Your sisters always turn to you for advice— can't you see that? They trust you to be cool and calm when you consider a problem.'

'Like now?' she said dryly.

'There's a difference between keeping your voice down, and being quiet and retiring, and the fact you don't shout the odds as loudly as your sisters doesn't mean you can't be heard. In fact, yours is the voice we all remember.'

Wrapping his arms around her, he drew Leila close so he could rest his face against her belly. His heart filled with love the moment he felt movement beneath him. It made him laugh; it made him smile. It was a miracle and he was part of it. Even more of a miracle was the fact that the babies and Leila had allowed him to feel after so many years of denying that pleasure. Thanks to them he could let loose his emotions and experience every life-changing moment to the full from now on. Reaching up, he drew Leila into his arms and kissed her, but what began as a tender expression of his love for Leila, and for their children, soon grew in passion. 'I'll never leave you again,' he pledged fiercely.

'Even if I want you to?' she challenged with a smile against his mouth.

'Even then.'

'Except for when you have to be away on business,' she guessed.

'I've only got a couple of appointments before Christmas and then I'm going to devote myself to you and the babies.'

'Really?'

'Give me your shopping list,' Raffa murmured.

'Most of what I want can be found right here,' she whispered. 'But if you're serious…'

'Absolutely.'

She could taste her tears on Raffa's mouth, but she could see her happiness reflected in his eyes. Like him, she had smothered her emotions, fearing them, but they had freed each other and she felt a settling and a peace inside her that she had never known before.

'I've never seen you like this,' Raffa said as she sniffed and laughed.

'You've never seen me this pregnant before.'

Raffa's sexy mouth slanted in a smile that warmed her through. 'I must admit two babies does account for some extra hormonal activity.'

Leila was just content to relish the strength of his arms and the sense of being safe.

'It's so good to be home finally, Leila.'

'And so surprising to want both the man and the baby,' she teased Raffa gently as he rested his brow against hers.

'Babies,' he reminded her wryly. 'What?' he queried lazily, brushing her lips with his.

'I thought we were going to have something to eat?'

'We are,' he confirmed. 'But not yet.'

'How am I supposed to resist you?'

'You're not.'

She held him off for a moment with both hands flat against his chest. 'Seriously. How can it ever work between us, Raffa, when we're worlds apart?'

'We're worlds colliding,' he argued, still teasing her lips with his.

'Why won't you admit I'm right?'

'Because I'm always right.'

She gave a small growl of warning to this, which made him smile. Leila was a passionate mother-to-be, high on hormones, which made her more beautiful than ever to him. She was like a lioness that, having tested her boundaries, had found them infinite, and had made the leap to freedom from a self-imposed cage. Quiet Leila had been temptation enough for him, but this new, bold version of the same woman was more than enough for him.

'You'll be a wonderful mother, Leila, but right now that's not uppermost in my mind.'

'How can you want me when I'm heavily pregnant, wearing my brother's cast-off work shirt?'

Her mention of Tyr threw him for a moment, and he longed to put her mind at rest, but a pledge was a pledge, and his honour was non-negotiable too.

'On you it could only be high fashion,' he teased, drawing a veil over the confidence he had sworn to keep for Tyr.

His body ached for Leila, and when he kissed her he felt a tremor of need run through her. Drawing back, he tested his theory. 'Still mad for sex?'

'What sort of question is that, Raffa? Of course I am.'

Losing no more time, he swung Leila into his arms. 'Your bedroom?'

'Under the eaves.'

'Perfect.'

It was perfect. Leila's bedroom was a warm, safe nest. If only he'd been able to think of her here while he'd been away, he wouldn't have worried about her half as much. No wonder she had wanted to come home to Skavanga. With the snow tumbling down outside the big windows that framed the lake, the mountains and the heavily snow-laden trees, it was paradise outside, and paradise inside. This was one haven he would never want to leave.

'Watch out! The room's too small for you,' she exclaimed as he ducked his head to avoid a beam.

'The room's perfect for me, Leila,' he said as he lowered her carefully onto the bed, kicked off his boots and lay down beside her.

'Mind reading's never been one of my many skills, but I do have others,' she said, toying with the buttons on his shirt.

'I remember them well,' he said as he started to undress her.

'Why are you smiling as you kiss me, Raffa?'

'You taste so good.'

'Anxiety and pregnancy taste good to you?'

'What are you anxious about, Leila?'

'That I can still do this—I mean, with this mega-sized bump.'

'We'll find a way,' he promised, kissing his way from her neck to her breasts. 'I was right—no anxiety here,' he confirmed, circling her nipples with his tongue before tugging on them gently.

'They're bigger.'

'They're lush and full and beautiful. Every part of you—'

'Is pregnant,' she said.

'Like I haven't noticed?' he murmured contentedly, kissing his way down to her belly.

'Will you stop that? I'm ugly—'

'A pregnant woman could never be called ugly. And you are particularly beautiful,' he insisted, nudging his way between her thighs.

'You can't—'

'I think you'll find I can...'

'Oh, yes… Oh, Raffa… Please—'

'Don't stop?' he queried with amusement, lifting his head. 'I've got no intention of stopping. You taste too good to stop—'

'Oh… I— Now! I can't hold on,' she wailed, lacing her fingers through his hair to keep him close.

'Let it go, baby— Just let it go—' He held her firmly. His tongue did the rest.

'That was amazing,' she managed, still convulsing as he kept her going with his hand.

'More?' he suggested.

'A lot more…'

'You've been missing this, I think,' he murmured, turning her so that now Leila had her back to him.

'So much—'

He laughed as he curled his body round her. 'Hang on,' he whispered, lifting her leg over his.

'How long do I have to hold on?' She gasped as he found her with his hand. 'I'm not sure I can—'

'Any time you like—'

She screamed her next release before he had even finished the sentence. He was gentle as he entered her—so gentle. It was good for him this way—like all the best sensations in the world woven together. Leila had curled up to allow him the best possible access and she was so ready for him—so warm, so tight, so wet. 'Tell me if I'm hurting you.'

'I'll tell you if you stop,' she growled.

He laughed softly, while Leila gasped out loud. He rocked into her gently, at the same time sheathing himself completely, maintaining the same steady rhythm with his hand while she thrust backwards onto him, dictating both the pace and force he was using. It wasn't long before she was on the edge again. He could feel the sudden tensing in her body—the awareness shimmering through her—the realisation that pleasure was on its way.

'Enjoy, baby,' he murmured. The slightest adjustment to the pressure and speed at which his finger was working was all it took to make it impossible for her to hold on, and as she let go with a series of wild cries of relief he increased the force and pace of his thrusts to prolong her pleasure for as long as he could.

They slept wrapped in each other's arms. Their discussion did not continue, as Leila had insisted it must do, straight after lovemaking—not that night, nor the next morning, or the next.

They lived the dream—the dream for both of them. Closeness without complications—without thought for the future. They were pushing difficult decisions aside, like where to live, and how to combine their two very different lives. They were together and that was all that mattered. They were getting to know each other better too. They were growing closer because of the sex, whereas in the past, sex had been an end in itself.

They padded around barefoot—sometimes even naked. Leila would cook something on the stove while he stood behind her with his hands loosely linked around her belly. Her calm essence healed him, while the food she cooked fuelled their lust. They took meals to bed—left others forgotten to grow cold as they feasted on each other.

He couldn't remember a time when he had ever been so happy, or so relaxed. And he couldn't bear to let this go. He couldn't envisage a time without Leila. He wasn't prepared to contemplate a future without her. But this timeless idyll had to end. They both knew it. He still had business commitments to fit in before everything closed down for Christmas, while Leila had insisted on working until the very last minute, and so, with less than a week to go before Christmas Day, he dropped her off at the mining museum on his way to the airport.

'We'll talk when I get back from New York. There's plenty of time,' he said confidently. 'The babies aren't due yet, so—'

'Plenty of time,' Leila confirmed, standing on tiptoe to kiss him goodbye.

If this past week of indulging themselves had achieved anything, it was to establish a new level of trust between them. They could do this. They were both strong individuals who could handle a long-distance relationship, and they would make sure their children didn't suffer because of it.

At least that was how he felt until he woke up one morning in an anonymous hotel somewhere in the world to find it was snowing, which reminded him of Skavanga. He could have been anywhere in the world. A luxury hotel was a luxury hotel and when he was away from Leila everywhere looked the same to him. He found himself longing for a small wood cabin on the shores of a lake, and a woman who for him had no equal. His meetings were over and all he could think about was Leila facing the run-up to their twins' birth on her own. It didn't have to be this way—for either of them.

He'd never had so much fun shopping. He'd never had fun shopping. It wasn't the type of thing he did, but today was different, and wherever he went his happiness was infectious. He had discounts pushed on him, encouraging him to buy ten times more than he had intended. He got back to the hotel, filed a flight plan for Skavanga and was airborne by late afternoon. He rented a Jeep at the airport and drove out to the cabin. He hadn't called Leila.

He hadn't warned her he was coming back. The feelings inside him didn't allow for half measures. This was either the biggest surprise she'd ever had or it was a dud.

She heard the engine and was hanging out of an upstairs window when he arrived. 'Raffa?' She sounded ecstatic. 'What are you doing?'

'Visiting a friend,' he called up, holding his feelings of elation on the shortest rein. 'I hope that friend hasn't been up a stepladder, decorating?' He tried and failed to adopt a stern tone. He was just so excited to see her—to hold her—to kiss her again.

'Your friend's been getting the nursery ready. What do you think?' She glanced over her shoulder, where he could see a set of ladders with tins of paint jostling for position on the top step.

'I think I'll have to paddle her backside, if that's what my friend's been up to—'

'Excellent,' she called down. 'Can't wait. The door's open—let yourself in.'

'You don't even lock the door round here?'

'I don't have too many barbarians calling—you're the first.'

She flew into his arms before he even had chance to step inside the house. 'Did you run down those stairs?' he demanded sternly, holding Leila at arm's length so he could stare into her eyes.

'No, I waddled down them—'

He didn't care how she got down the stairs, just that she had got down them safely and was in his arms again. Dragging her close, he kissed her. If this was what it felt like to come home, he was coming home every day from now on.

'I've missed you so much,' she exclaimed, searching his eyes as she gripped him as if her life depended on it.

'I've only been away a few days—'

'Too long,' she interrupted him fiercely, resting her cheek against his heavy jacket.

'Come on,' he said, wrapping her inside the jacket. 'Let's go inside before you catch cold. It's freezing out here.'

'You think?' she demanded cheekily, staring up at him. 'I'm really hot.'

'So you are.' He acted surprised, and then dragged her close as he ushered the woman he loved into the house.

CHAPTER FOURTEEN

'No. You don't do anything, Leila. This is a time for you to rest, so I do it all,' he insisted, having stripped down to his top and jeans after bringing all his booty into the open-plan living room.

'You do it all?' Leila demanded cheekily as he rifled through the bags. 'Haven't we been here before?'

'But never at the cooker—'

She laughed. 'Can you cook?' she demanded, planting her hands on her hips.

'I can,' he said as he slammed a cookery book written by a hot chef on the scrubbed pine table. 'All I have to be able to do is read and keep a handle on the time.'

'Multitasking?' She looked dubious.

'I'm not your typical man—remember?'

She laughed. 'So you're definitely promising something more than tins and fries?'

'No tins. No fries,' he confirmed. 'Just really great organic food direct from the market for the mother-to-be—'

'And you're going to do *everything* for me?' Leila confirmed as if she needed this in writing before he stood a chance of making her believe him.

'*Señorita*—' He made her a mock bow. 'I'm going to make Christmas for you.'

'And what do I have to do?' She lifted a brow.

'You have to stand there and look pretty—'

'Pretty fat? Pretty awful?'

'Pretty pregnant,' he argued, dragging her into his arms. 'And you've got paint on your nose,' he murmured, brushing her lips with his.

'Sorry—'

'Don't be.' He held her at arm's length. 'Have you been eating while I've been away?' She looked pale, he thought.

'Of course I have.'

'Not convinced, Leila. But I'm going to make it right. Break out the beer for me, the juice for you—'

'And you'll get cooking?' Her smile lit up her face. 'This I have to see.'

His heart soared as she laughed. 'This you're going to see, *señorita*. And while we're on the subject of making Christmas—you haven't done too badly yourself. You've added some more decorations.'

'Do you like it?' she said, glancing round at the traditional Scandinavian ornaments. 'I haven't overdone it?'

'Are you kidding?' He grinned. 'Christmas can never be overdone.'

There was a big pine tree festooned with tiny bells and flags to one side of the crackling fire, and while many of the decorations appeared to be recently home-made, others were a bit battered, and obviously much loved after many outings. There was a lot of red and white fabric, which looked great against the pine walls of the cabin. The hems of the curtains, the cushions, the throws, were all heavily embroidered with dainty, though intricate, cross-stitch.

'My grandmother's work,' Leila explained, seeing

him looking at it. 'They don't come out very often, but I changed them especially for you.'

There were hearts and bells and Santa and Mrs Claus on the window ledges, and on the table an arrangement of candles, moss and berries. It was a homely setting and one that warmed him through. 'This is quite something to live up to,' he observed as he rolled up his sleeves. 'I'd better get cooking—'

'Yes, you better had. Would you like a glass of eggnog to go with that beer?'

'I think I should keep a clear head, don't you?'

Before she could answer him, he dragged her into his arms. 'Happy Christmas, Leila Skavanga. Do you have any idea how much I love you?'

'You love me?'

'Yes, I do. Of course I do!'

She smiled cheekily at him. 'Then I hope you can prove it again and again.'

'In so many ways,' he promised softly. Staring deep into Leila's eyes, he sank into her calm, loving expression. He'd missed her so much.

'Your last Christmas without babies,' he commented wryly, pulling back to start cooking. 'Make the most of it—it's sleepless nights from here on in.'

'I can't wait.'

'It will be hard work.'

'I'm looking forward to that too.'

And he wanted to be part of it—now more than ever.

He surprised himself with the array of tempting dishes he produced, and there was Christmas Day to come yet. 'Who knows what miracles I can conjure up, now I've hit my stride.'

'Modest as always, Raffa—but I have to admit, this is delicious.' Leila laughed as she tucked in.

He hummed and adopted a thoughtful look. 'Maybe I should take cooking up as a profession?'

Cocking her head to one side, Leila disagreed with this proposition. 'You can't do that. We need you down at the mine.'

'Then I'll take over the café.'

'Oh, no, you won't.' She worked a frown. 'Stealing my customers from the museum? We'd never get the women out of there if you were running it.'

'And while we're on the subject of *your* museum, Señorita Skavanga,' he interrupted, seizing his chance. 'You have to stop working there soon.'

'When the babies come, I'll stop.'

'Take care you don't give birth during one of the tours. It would give a whole new meaning to "If you'd like to follow me…"'

'Bet no one would take me up on that one.'

'Here—Leila. Taste.'

'Hmm—delicious,' she exclaimed, but quickly returned to her chosen subject. 'I'll know when it's right to stop working, Raffa. I'm a good couple of weeks away.'

'Don't I have any say in this? Oh, yeah, wait a moment, I do,' he drawled as Leila tipped up her chin to challenge him. 'And if I say you stop work right after we celebrate Christmas, so you can put your feet up over New Year—'

'You've got it all worked out, haven't you, Raffa?'

Bringing their plates to the table, he laid them down with a flourish. 'I usually do—'

'And so do I,' Leila assured him, her lips set in a stubborn line. 'And I am going to stop work when my body tells me it's time to stop work, and not a moment sooner.'

'Are we playing whose will is stronger?' he suggested as he spooned some of the deliciously aromatic paella onto her plate.

'That's easy—I win,' she assured him. 'This is delicious, by the way.'

'So you accept I can multitask?'

'I accept you're an exceptional man, Señor Leon—but that doesn't mean I have to do everything you say—'

'In bed or out of it?'

'That's a loaded question from a very bad man.'

'Yes, it is,' he agreed. 'More paella?'

'I could never get enough of this.'

'Excellent—fill your mouth and be quiet for a second, because I've got a very important question to ask you.'

'What are you doing on your knees? Did I drop some food on the floor?'

'Señorita Skavanga…Leila…will you do me the honour of agreeing to become my wife?'

She froze and stared at him. And then had to chew double fast and swallow before she could exclaim, 'Are you serious?'

'Would I be down here on the floor for any other reason?'

'It does seem unlikely,' she agreed, shooting him a wicked look. Then sliding off the stool, she joined him on the floor, kneeling in front of him, which was no small feat in Leila's condition. Linking fingers with him, she stared into his eyes. 'Raffa Leon, will you do me the honour of becoming my husband?'

'In the interest of harmony and equality? Yes.'

'I love you very much,' she whispered as he kissed her hands.

'And I love you, Leila Skavanga.' Leaning very far forward indeed so he could reach past the bump, he kissed the woman he loved again…and again.

EPILOGUE

IT STARTED WITHOUT WARNING. One minute Leila was sitting across from him telling him some crazy anecdote from her childhood, and the next her face was frozen with shock.

'Leila?' He was out of his seat and round her side of the table in a heartbeat.

'The babies—' She panted the words out. 'Raffa— Call an ambulance!'

'I'm taking you to the hospital,' he stated calmly. 'I'll call ahead to warn them we're on our way—'

'Raffa— Raffa! I can't—'

Grabbing a couple of throws from the sofa, he wrapped them around her. Lifting her, he picked up his keys on his way across the room, but by the time they reached the front door it was clear they weren't going anywhere.

This was one time neither of them could control the situation. Plucking the phone out of his pocket, he called the emergency number, trying to subdue his fears. He'd faced guns and knives in the course of his travels when he was searching for gems in some of the world's wildest places, but he had never known fear like this in his life. The thought of losing Leila—

He might as well be dead too. He would do anything,

anything to keep her safe, but the babies weren't going to wait for his team of experts.

'Stay on the line,' he told the paramedic as he shouldered his way into Leila's room. 'I might need you to talk me through this.'

Not only couldn't he control the speed of this birth, he needed help. And where Leila was concerned, he was grateful for every word of advice they could give him.

He laid her down on the bed. She reached for his hand and kissed it. 'I'm so glad you're here with me, Raffa.'

'I won't leave you for a second—unless the paramedic tells me I have to go fetch something,' he qualified, realising that for once in his life he really didn't know best. The thought of Leila giving birth alone to twins in an isolated cabin, however cosy and safe she might think it, racked him with guilt. What if he hadn't been here? He should have insisted she move to town. He should have hired help— Damn it to hell! He should have arrived in Skavanga sooner—

'Raffa?'

'Sorry—' His cursing had been both forceful and eloquent. 'I don't think the twins can hear me yet.'

She managed a laugh. 'You're going to make a terrible father if you swear all the time.'

'I'm already a terrible partner. I don't know what I was thinking leaving you here on your own so close to the birth.'

'We thought we knew when the babies were arriving. I was stubborn. I told you to go. I was so certain I knew exactly when they were coming.'

The babies cut her off again before she could say anything more. Like him, they were impatient—impatient to be born. He listened closely to the advice the paramedic was giving him. 'I've got to grab a few things, but I'll be right back—'

'I'm not going anywhere, Raffa.'

Leila was smiling bravely, but all the ghosts from the past hit him at once as he stared down at her. If he failed her— If he failed her now—

No chance. There was no chance that would happen. He recited the list so she could tell him where to find everything. 'Here—take the phone and keep speaking to the paramedic,' he suggested, already halfway out of the door. 'They're on their way—'

Her face turned anxious. 'They might not get here soon enough, Raffa.'

'But I'm here,' he reassured her, 'and the local medics are flying in by air ambulance, so they won't take long.'

As she sank back on the pillows he realised Leila had turned his life upside down. And he thanked God for it.

He thanked God even more heartily when the sound of rotor blades drowned out the sound of the kettle boiling. He would walk on hot coals for Leila, but the thought of risking her life or those of the twins by making some beginner's mistake during the delivery was a calamity he refused to consider. One baby, maybe. But two? He'd do it. Of course he'd do it, but knowing medical assistance was on its way had lifted his spirits and made it possible for him to look forward to the birth of his children with excitement and happiness, rather than the dragging fear that had dogged him since he had first learned Leila was pregnant. Scrawling a note for the medics, he attached it to the wreath outside the front door.

He took the stairs two at a time. So much for his relief at the quick response of the medical team! The first baby was already on its way. There was no mistaking the father of this impatient, strong-willed boy. He was wrapping the youngest member of the Leon dynasty in a towel and placing him in Leila's arms as the paramedics joined them in the room. He stood back immediately to let the professionals do their job.

'Raffa, you're wonderfully calm,' Leila managed on a shaking breath as the second twin made her noisy entrance into her world. 'I couldn't have done any of this without you.'

'You could probably have done all of it without me, but I'm glad you didn't have to. You shouldn't have to,' he murmured, studying the face of his firstborn as the paramedics checked his son's tiny baby sister over. 'And I don't think either of us had a choice. These babies were coming when they decided the time was right, with or without our agreement.'

'Happy Christmas, Raffa,' she murmured as the paramedics loaded her onto a stretcher.

'Happy Christmas, mouse.'

The look they exchanged was full of love and peace, and the promise of a happy future together with their children, though Leila was no more a mouse these days than he was a restless adventurer. She had given him the home he'd always longed for, while he had only to stand back and watch Leila grow in confidence, he reflected with amusement. Leila had turned out to be every bit as feisty as her sisters. Like Britt and Eva, she was a true Skavanga Diamond, but, as far as he was concerned, Leila was the jewel in the crown.

* * * * *

#3233 SHEIKH'S SCANDAL
The Chatsfield
by Lucy Monroe

The world's media is buzzing as brooding Sheikh Sayed and his harem take up residence at the exclusive Chatsfield Hotel...but an even bigger scandal threatens to break when a stolen night with chambermaid Liyah Amari results in an unexpected complication....

#3234 THE ONLY WOMAN TO DEFY HIM
by Carol Marinelli

Personal assistant Alina Ritchi finds her defiance ignited under the powerful gaze of legendary playboy Demyan Zukov. But when every shared touch sizzles, how long can Alina keep saying 'no' when her body wants to scream 'yes'?

#3235 GAMBLING WITH THE CROWN
Heirs to the Throne of Kyr
by Lynn Raye Harris

When Sheikh Kadir al Hassan promotes long-suffering assistant Emily Bryant to royal bride, he's convinced she'll be deemed so unsuitable he'll successfully avoid the crown. But one kiss forces Kadir to make the ultimate choice: his desert duty, or Emily!

#3236 ONE NIGHT TO RISK IT ALL
by Maisey Yates

Dutiful Rachel Holt has never put a foot wrong...until she reaches for one electrifying night with notorious Greek tycoon Alexios Christofides. But *this* one night has great consequences for them both, especially when Rachel realizes Alex's true identity!

HPCNM0414RA

#3237 SECRETS OF A RUTHLESS TYCOON
by Cathy Williams
There's one thing Leo Spencer's luxurious lifestyle can't give him—the truth about his past. His search for answers leads him to Brianna Sullivan, hidden in the Irish countryside, where she soon proves to be a distraction he never anticipated....

#3238 THE FORBIDDEN TOUCH OF SANGUARDO
by Julia James
Self-made millionaire Rafael Sanguardo *always* gets what he wants...and he wants Celeste Philips. Celeste knows she shouldn't fall for Rafael's practiced charm, yet the more her head tells her to walk away...the more she craves his forbidden touch!

#3239 A CLASH WITH CANNAVARO
by Elizabeth Power
Italian billionaire Emiliano Cannavaro is determined to regain custody of his orphaned nephew from Lauren Westwood—a woman he believes is after only one thing. But innocent Lauren won't give up without a fight—and it promises to be explosive!

#3240 THE TRUTH ABOUT DE CAMPO
by Jennifer Hayward
Matteo de Campo wants to secure a multi-million dollar deal with Quinn's family's company—which means she mustn't fall for his enticing appeal! But when Quinn glimpses his inner demons, she's determined to discover just *who* the real Matteo is....

REQUEST YOUR FREE BOOKS!

2 FREE NOVELS PLUS
2 FREE GIFTS!

YES! Please send me 2 FREE Harlequin Presents® novels and my 2 FREE gifts (gifts are worth about $10). After receiving them, if I don't wish to receive any more books, I can return the shipping statement marked "cancel." If I don't cancel, I will receive 6 brand-new novels every month and be billed just $4.30 per book in the U.S. or $4.99 per book in Canada. That's a saving of at least 14% off the cover price! It's quite a bargain! Shipping and handling is just 50¢ per book in the U.S. and 75¢ per book in Canada.* I understand that accepting the 2 free books and gifts places me under no obligation to buy anything. I can always return a shipment and cancel at any time. Even if I never buy another book, the two free books and gifts are mine to keep forever.

106/306 HDN FVRK

Name _____ (PLEASE PRINT) _____

Address _____ Apt. # _____

City _____ State/Prov. _____ Zip/Postal Code _____

Signature (if under 18, a parent or guardian must sign)

Mail to the **Harlequin® Reader Service:**
IN U.S.A.: P.O. Box 1867, Buffalo, NY 14240-1867
IN CANADA: P.O. Box 609, Fort Erie, Ontario L2A 5X3

**Are you a current subscriber to Harlequin Presents books
and want to receive the larger-print edition?
Call 1-800-873-8635 or visit www.ReaderService.com.**

* Terms and prices subject to change without notice. Prices do not include applicable taxes. Sales tax applicable in N.Y. Canadian residents will be charged applicable taxes. Offer not valid in Quebec. This offer is limited to one order per household. Not valid for current subscribers to Harlequin Presents books. All orders subject to credit approval. Credit or debit balances in a customer's account(s) may be offset by any other outstanding balance owed by or to the customer. Please allow 4 to 6 weeks for delivery. Offer available while quantities last.

Your Privacy—The Harlequin® Reader Service is committed to protecting your privacy. Our Privacy Policy is available online at www.ReaderService.com or upon request from the Harlequin Reader Service.

We make a portion of our mailing list available to reputable third parties that offer products we believe may interest you. If you prefer that we not exchange your name with third parties, or if you wish to clarify or modify your communication preferences, please visit us at www.ReaderService.com/consumerschoice or write to us at Harlequin Reader Service Preference Service, P.O. Box 9062, Buffalo, NY 14269. Include your complete name and address.

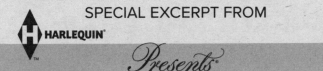
*Harlequin Presents welcomes you to the world of
The Chatsfield—synonymous with style, spectacle...
and scandal! Read on for an exclusive extract from
Lucy Monroe's stunning story SHEIKH'S SCANDAL.
The first in an exciting new eight-book series:*
THE CHATSFIELD.

* * *

THE guest elevators at The Chatsfield hotel in London were spacious by any definition, but the confined area *felt* small to Aaliyah Amari.

"You're not very Western in your outlook," she said, trying to ignore the unfamiliar desires and emotions roiling through her.

"I am the heart of Zeena Sahra—should my people and their ways not be the center of mine?"

She didn't like how much his answer touched her. To cover her reaction she waved her hand between the two of them and said, "This isn't the way of Zeena Sahra."

"You are so sure?" he asked.

"Yes."

He laughed, the honest sound of genuine amusement more compelling than even the uninterrupted regard of the extremely handsome man. "You are not like other women."

"You're the emir."

"You are saying other women are awed by me."

She gave him a wry look and said drily, "You're not conceited at all, are you?"

"Is it conceit to recognize the truth?"

She shook her head. Even arrogant, she found this man irresistible, and she had the terrible suspicion he knew it, too.

Unsure how she'd got there, she felt the wall of the elevator at her back. Sayed's body was so close his outer robes brushed her. Her breath came out on a shocked gasp.

He brushed her lower lip with his fingertip. "Your mouth is luscious."

"This is a bad idea."

"Is it?" he asked, his head dipping toward hers.

"Yes. I'm not part of the amenities."

"I know." His tone rang with sincerity.

"I don't do elevator romps," she clarified, just in case he didn't get it.

Something flared in his dark gaze and Sayed stepped back, shaking his head. "I apologize, Miss Amari. I do not know what came over me."

"I'm sure you're used to women falling all over you," she offered by way of an explanation.

He frowned. "Is that meant to be a sop to my ego or a slam against it?"

"Neither?"

He shook his head again, as if trying to clear it.

She wondered if it worked. She would be grateful for a technique that brought back her own usual way of thinking, unobscured by this unwelcome and unfamiliar desire.

* * *

Step into the gilded world of THE CHATSFIELD!
Where secrets and scandal lurk behind every door...

Reserve your room in May 2014!